A deep sense of foreboding filled Jessica.

"What is the matter, Alec?" she asked quietly, preparing herself for the shock she knew without a doubt was coming her way. He didn't reply at first.

"My ex-wife arrived from New York this morning."

The news took Jessica completely by surprise. "Why?" she asked weakly.

"She needs me."

"I s-see," she whispered for lack of something else to say.

"No, you don't," he muttered. His derision cut into her, making her flinch.

"Listen, Jess . . ." he began huskily. "I want to try to explain something to you."

Jessica knew then with a sickening certainty that Alec was about to shatter her life.

D0724772

Michelle Reid lives in Cheshire, England, dividing her time between being a full-time housewife and mother looking after her husband and two teenage daughters and writing. She says her family takes it very well, fending for themselves until she "comes up for air," though she's not sure which they find harder to put up with, being cleaned and polished when she's in a housekeeping mood or being ignored when she's absorbed in writing and tends to forget they're alive! She has a passion for fresh air and exercise, which she gets at the local tennis club.

Eye of
Heaven
Michelle Reid

Harlequin Books

TORONTO • NEW YORK • LONDON
AMSTERDAM • PARIS • SYDNEY • HAMBURG

Original hardcover edition published in 1988
by Mills & Boon Limited

ISBN 0-373-02994-2

Harlequin Romance first edition July 1989

CHAPTER ONE

'I'M telling you, Teddy, I've had enough!'

The atmosphere in the rear of the chauffeur-driven limousine was fraught, to say the least: the beautiful Jessica Christhanson huddling into a thick fur coat, shivering despite the efficiency of the car's heating system, while Edward G. Thirsten was trying his best to appear at ease, in the faint hope that his careless manner would rub off on the overwrought actress beside him.

'I want to go home, have a bath—wash his filthy touch from my skin!' Jessica shuddered. 'What he did to me was close to...' She couldn't say it, swallowing hard on the unutterable word. 'I just can't take any more today,' she finished on a shaky whisper.

'This *one* last stop, sweetie.' Teddy sounded his usual superficial self. Near rape, it seemed, did not constitute a good enough reason to alter the day's agenda. 'Let the nice Alec Stedman take his pretty pics, then you can go home and soak in your hot tub—and forget about the lot of us for a whole month! Think of it,' he trilled. 'One teeny weeny hour of nice Jessie smiles and the pretty pics will be taken—click, click, click! Otherwise, sweetie,' he added slyly, 'you will only have to turn out tomorrow to do the session.'

His trump card, Jessica noted bitterly. Teddy always had one. He may spend ninety-nine per cent of his life playing the idiot, but it was a blind, put up to hide the real man-eating shark who lurked beneath, which was, of course, why Teddy was the most successful theatrical agent in the business.

But that meant nothing to Jessica Christhanson at this moment in time; she was too angry and upset to care who or what Teddy was. 'Can't you understand?' she

5

cried, turning to glare at him, incredible blue eyes glinting with near-tears. 'I can't take any more! My skin is crawling with that—*animal's* touch...and there is no way I can take another manhandling today!'

'But Stedman's *cool*!' Teddy rushed in to proclaim. '*Cool-cool-cool!* Don't maul the ladies like Blake, don't even touch 'em if he can help it. He's cool, Jess,' he repeated for the umpteenth teeth-clenching time. 'Genius in his field, but hates models, hates 'em!' Teddy's snappily dressed frame shuddered in eloquent example of the genius's supposed reaction to women. 'Ugh!' he added for good measure. 'Hates 'em. Won't even touch your poor, unhappy skin.'

'I'm not a model,' she muttered.

'God, no! Beautiful Actress Lady,' he agreed with fawning verve. 'But same thing to him, sweetie. Lady with a face. Lady with glamour. Lady on the fantasy merry-go-round.' He shrugged again, sandy brows twitching ruefully. 'Stedman can't stand 'em—takes super pics of 'em—but can't stand 'em.'

'And what has he got against 'em—*them*?' she sighed, impatiently, because Teddy's affected way of speaking was beginning to rub off on her.

'A wife, that's what,' said Teddy. 'An ex-wife, anyway. Model—*La bella!*' He kissed the beautifully manicured tips of his fingers. 'Remember Tracy Lopez—yeah? Mr Cameraman discovered her. Trained her, primped and prettied her, married her, took his super pics of her and sent her soaring to the top—then watched her walk out on him when the big fat man with the big fat cigar came along, promising to make her into a film star!' His acid mockery made Jessica wince. 'Never forgave her, never forgave the whole female race, 'specially glamour ones. But he's the best in his business,' he declared. 'Has a *cheeky* little trick of making the ladies look special— better than they really are! Oh, not *you*, sweetie!' he quickly inserted, sending her one of his silly clown smiles. 'Can't improve on perfection, you know, it...'

'Oh, do shut up, Teddy,' Jessica drawled wearily. 'I may be angry and disgusted and fed up, but I'm not stupid! I got the gist early on.'

'Oh—quite.' He actually looked offended! The devious devil knew exactly what he was doing, playing on her sympathy. Everyone who knew him knew the mortification you felt on offending the inoffensive Teddy.

'Tracy Lopez, you say?' Teddy nodded, stricken-eyed, mouth obediently tight shut.

Jessica had heard of her—who hadn't? she thought drily. At one time, her face could be seen on almost every advertisement for beauty products. Not so much now, though. She frowned, trying to remember when the famous Tracy Lopez face had ceased looking back at her from wherever she happened to glance. She had that dark and lusty kind of attraction men went weak over... It was no wonder Alec Stedman was off women! I mean, she thought bitterly, who could follow that?

'Don't you dare leave me alone for a second, Teddy!' she warned, as a way of giving in.

His hands went up placatingly. 'Not even to take a leak!' he promised, trying hard not to shriek in delight.

Despite her mood, Jessica had to smile. Only Teddy would say something like that—only Teddy would dare!

Conversation died then, Teddy because he knew when to leave well alone, Jessica because her recent ordeal at the lecherous hands of Joel Blake had shaken her. In the five years since she'd left drama school and clinched her first acting role, she had never once come up against that kind of sexual coercion. She had only agreed to read for Blake's latest film as a special favour to Teddy. The big American producer had asked specifically for her, and, as Teddy had rightly pointed out, you can't afford to offend men of his standing in the profession. It never even occurred to her, until it was too late, just what the ageing old roué was intending until he pulled her down on the couch and began mauling her. She could almost laugh—albeit scornfully—at her own naïveté. His hungry expression should have alerted her the moment she had entered his suite, but it hadn't. Physical and mental exhaustion had certainly dulled her instincts. Fancy getting caught by the casting-couch routine! she mocked herself bitterly. And thank God Teddy had been on hand to save her from a potentially nasty situation. What had actually taken place before Teddy had barged in on them had been enough!

'Forget Blake,' Teddy advised, reading her like an open book as usual. 'One of life's degenerates. Thinks he's God's gift to women…got a personality problem there,' he opined consideringly. 'Needs it seeing to. Can't go around believing you're Peter Pan when you ain't any more. Can't——'

'Shut up, Teddy.'

'Oh——' She had offended him again. 'Yes, of course. Didn't think, didn't mean to…'

'Shut—up,' she repeated with quiet clarity. It worked this time. His parted mouth closed over the words itching for expression, and stayed shut. Jessica gave him a look of grim satisfaction, then turned her attention inwards, trying to build slowly on her sadly depleted self-confidence in preparation for the next ordeal, which she knew the hour-long photographic session was bound to be.

'We're here.'

Jessica became aware of their surroundings with a faint surprise showing on her face as the car turned in through a pair of high wooden gates and began crunching up a fine shingle driveway towards what appeared to be a private mansion house.

It was old—early Victorian at a guess, built in red brick, with deep sash bay windows and imposing gables. Green, yellow and silver ivy clambered over the walls. For a place of work, she mused idly, Alec Stedman's premises had a distinctly lived-in look about them; she'd even spied a swing hanging from an ancient pear tree towards the rear of the house, just before the car swerved to a neat stop outside the front porch. Her mind instantly conjured up a picture of some sweet Victorian young lady seated on the swing, her white gown billowing, hat ribbons fluttering as her beau pushed her gently to and fro, pear blossom hanging heavy on the tree branches.

Pretty, she thought, cleansing—almost.

The chauffeur opened her door, standing respectfully to one side to allow her to alight. Jessica drew in a deep breath and forced her reluctant limbs to move, drawing her coat further around her, collar turned up, trapping the long length of her pale blonde hair inside. The incredible fairness of her skin hid its true bloodless state. She looked what she was—a very special, very successful and beautiful young woman. Only those who knew her well would be able to note the odd tightness around her small jaw, the dullness in her normally vibrant blue eyes.

Teddy was beside her in an instant, taking her arm in a reassuring grip. Tall, with a sylph-like slimness, he was a man who used every trick known to him to appear a rather vain and insignificant fool—which he was not. His suit was slate-grey and impeccable, his shirt, which was white and pure silk, open at the throat to show off the dark red silk cravat he was favouring today, complete with diamond pin. His shoes were grey and white spats, his brimmed hat an exact match to the pale grey coat he wore casually about his shoulders. Only those grey-blue eyes, for ever shaded by lazy lids, hinted at the real shrewd and ruthless businessman he was, and Jessica was glad of his presence just now. Actress she might be, and she would play this part to the best of her ability, but inside she was a mass of angry emotions. Just one spark would set them off and she knew she would go up like a touch-paper.

One of Teddy's immaculate and beringed fingers went languidly to press the call bell. There was a muffled 'Woof!' from the other side of the solid wood doors, the sound of shuffling feet and a curt rebuke, then the door was opening inwards to reveal a tiny old woman

with silver hair and the kind of face Jessica associated
with someone's dear old aunty.

'Miss Christhanson?' She smiled warmly at Jessica,
who nodded and smiled in return. Then the old woman
was drawing the door wider, and at the same time levelling her gaze on Teddy, and her whole manner took
on a complete metamorphosis. 'Well,' she huffed out,
one gnarled and swollen hand holding the door while
the other held on to the collar of a huge Old English
sheep-dog. 'I thought I'd seen everything pass through
this door,' she went on, shaking her snowy head as she
looked him slowly up and down. 'But you, young man,
take the trophy!'

Jessica held back the desire to laugh, while Teddy sent
the old woman one of his bright, trivial smiles, giving
the appearance that the criticism had washed clean over
him. 'Thank you,' he said blandly, and stepped into the
hall, eyeing the huge dog with distaste as he drew Jessica
with him.

The dog, as if in retaliation, shook his shaggy coat,
peered contemptuously at Teddy through his shaggy
fringe, then, on a snort that sounded to Jessica suspiciously like scorn, ambled away to flop lazily down
across the bottom of the stairs.

'The studio is upstairs,' the woman informed them.
Jessica glanced around her surroundings, quiet, salubri-
ous surroundings, meant for living and feeling at home
in. 'Samson!' A well padded thigh was slapped
commandingly.

The dog, hearing his name called in that stern fashion,
lifted his scruffy head—only the evidence of a shiny black
nose said it was his head—and gave the laziest and
huskiest 'woof' Jessica had ever heard, then plonked his
head back down again in an outright refusal to move.

The old lady glowered at him. 'Come out of the way,
you stupid old dog!' she muttered. He didn't budge, and
on a huff of impatience she shuffled over to him, tutting
and muttering about big lazy oafs who blocked stairways
and left hairs all over the place. The dog observed her

approach, his tail beginning to brush from side to side on the polished wood floor. Another doggy 'woof' of refusal brought him an answering slap to his rear end and he got up, taking his time, yawning and stretching, shaking out his amazing coat. Then he turned to lick affectionately the hand that slapped him, before ambling off towards the back of the house.

The old face was kind again when it turned back to them, her fondness of the dog very evident. 'Upstairs to the first floor, turn left along the gallery,' she directed them. 'At the other end you'll see a pair of doors. Knock and wait until you're invited to go in,' she warned, 'or Mr Alec will have your hide. I would take you up myself, only then Alec would have *my* hide for climbing the stairs.' Her smile was pure mischief, then she was shuffling off the same way as the dog had gone. It was only then that Jessica noticed the limp and the stiffness of her right hip. Arthritis, she guessed sadly.

'Nice place,' Teddy murmured, indicating that she precede him up the wide stairway.

Jessica made no reply, her hand still clutching her coat to her. Inside she felt ice-cold with lingering shock, while outside her skin still prickled with the loathing of Joel Blake's clammy touch. No matter how pleasing to the eye were Alec Stedman's premises, she was wishing herself a million miles away just now.

The gallery the old lady had referred to was long and imposing, the whole length of it covered in old masters, large gold-framed paintings with severe haughty faces glaring disapprovingly down at them as they passed.

Alec Stedman's ancestors? she wondered drily. Not an encouraging proposition; most of them looked capable of anything disreputable! The notion brought back the image of a leering Joel Blake, and she veered dizzily away from it, refusing to so much as glance at the portraits again, in case they further battered her bruised emotions.

Teddy knocked on the doors while she huddled deep into her full-length fur coat, cold even though the house was quite warm. There was a long pause, then one of the doors flew inwards, startling both of them, to reveal a man the size of a giant, with a pair of the strangest yellow eyes Jessica had ever encountered.

Good grief! Jessica thought. Helios, the sun god, personified!

He stood somewhere above six foot three; his tawny hair streaked with gold, lay thick and silky around his well shaped head. His features, like carefully honed rock, showed a man who wore his character like a warning to all comers. Strength, it said, of mind and body. Those strange eyes were framed by thick, golden lashes, his nose was almost but not quite haughty, but his mouth revealed the sensitivity that must be in him some-where—or he wouldn't be the renowned photographer he was, would he? Jessica wondered breathlessly. It was wide and full, and had a tendency to curve upwards at the corners, even when he was angry—like now.

His skin glowed like polished gold, gleaming at her from the gap in his casually fastened shirt, at his throat and chest, where golden whorls of pale body hair curled in virile profusion. He was long and lean, with the hard, packed muscles needed to complement his imposing stature.

He was staring coldly at her, eyeing her up and down before dismissing her with a cynical quirk of that wide mouth and turning his attention on Teddy, leaving her feeling as if she had just experienced the absolute op-posite of rape, and she reeled from the blow, wondering dazedly which incident had affected her the worse!

'You're late,' he snarled.

Golden-voiced, too, Jessica noted disturbingly. Even in anger, he purred like a lion.

'Sorry, sorry, sorry.' Teddy put up placating hands, his expression one of his very best 'idiot' looks. 'Got held up. Nasty business at last appointment. Jessica's cross, I'm cross—you're cross! Rotten day all round,' he finished on a shrug.

Alec—she presumed this was Alec Stedman, though he hadn't bothered introducing himself—was staring at

Teddy's expression of woebegone innocence with narrowed eyes, wondering, no doubt, as everyone did on their first meeting with Edward G. Thirsten, what the hell he was being treated to.

But behind that idiocy lurked a mind that could burn like a laser, if pushed, as Alec Stedman would find out if he tried putting it to the test—which he seemed to be considering. Teddy could change from toad to tiger in the blink of an eye. It was what made him such a good manager of people like her, people of the entertainment world. His chameleon act had certainly taken Joel Blake by surprise. One minute he had been smiling like an idiot in bliss as he left them alone to do the reading, the next he was back in the room and dragging Joel Blake off her, and ruining that famous profile with a punch that sent the oversexed director flying against a wall. Then, while he helped Jessica up, straightened her gaping clothes and smoothed her tumbled hair, he used his tongue on what was left of Blake's ego. They had left the man still cringing in a corner, wondering no doubt, what had happened to nice, meek—if annoyingly effusive—Teddy?

'You cold, lady?'

Jessica jumped, her gaze going up to Alec Stedman's in startled surprise. He was looking back at her with disdain, flicking a contemptuous look at her thick fur coat and the way she clutched it tensely to her throat. 'Or are you huddling inside that dead cat because you're wearing nothing beneath? If so——' he went on before she could make a gasping reply '—I'd better warn you, I don't do nudes, not even ones packaged as provocatively as you.'

'Naughty, naughty!' Teddy jumped in to wag an incredibly long finger under the other man's arrogant nose. He was smiling, as always, but there was a hint of steel in his voice. 'People with expensive cameras shouldn't throw insults, you know,' he happily misquoted. 'Bad for them, bad for everyone, bad thing all around...'

'Let's go, Teddy.' Jessica grabbed his arm, turning on her heel to face the way they had just come, her intention clear to both men. She wasn't staying here to be insulted by this arrogant waste of good male flesh. Teddy could use his smooth tongue as much as he liked, but she had had enough!

But Teddy had other ideas, and there was a dangerous light glinting in his eyes as he stalled her departure by turning her back to face the hateful Alec Stedman. 'Let's go inside, shall we?' he blithely trilled, but his hand came over her cold one where it rested on his arm, letting her know he was well aware of how she was feeling and how he was here to support her.

His glance brushed briefly and blankly with the other man, then they were stepping through the doors and into the giant's parlour.

It was a huge room, white-walled with long sash windows at either end. Every available bit of floor space was occupied by some piece of expensive equipment or other. Its walls lined with props—old and modern—it looked like the wings of a theatre, the ceiling like a stage ceiling, with pulleys and spotlights of all shapes, colours and sizes.

Only one area of the room was clear of debris, and that was where a raised platform stood, lit by several spots. Three people stood about, all busy fiddling with something mechanical, either lighting or expensive photographic equipment. The doors closed behind them, and Jessica felt the return of her inner turmoil. She could really do without this today.

'Draw the blinds.' The command went up, and a young man with long, lank hair and bottle bottoms for glasses jumped to carry out the order. 'Take that coat off, lady.' That was to her, Jessica realised with a shiver. 'Sandra—move Big Bessie away.' Big Bessie, it seemed was a crane-mounted camera, which a thin girl slid across the room with the aid of a computerised control panel. 'You——' he pointed to Teddy '—get yourself out of

my viewing range and forget you're here 'til I remind
you. The coat, lady,' he said again.

'Miss Christhanson,' she corrected, unmoving, looking
at him with such icy disdain that it stopped him in his
tracks. He stared back, seeing her, she guessed, for the
first time as a living, breathing person. 'Miss
Christhanson,' she repeated slowly and concisely. 'I am
a person, not a prop.'

A sudden silence fell about the room. Alec Stedman
was looking at her narrowly, those strange yellow eyes
regarding her in a wholly new and challenging way,
stretching out the tense silence until it began buzzing in
her ears, sending a soft flush creeping along her skin.

Something sparked between them, something so violently sexual that Jessica stiffened in rejection of it.
Yellow eyes darkened as he, too, recognised that unwanted spark, then he was bowing sardonically to her
and his mockery stung her heated skin.

'Miss Christhanson,' he drawled, softly, so silkily that
she quivered, 'would you mind removing your coat?'
American. It only hit her then, that he was an American,
with a soft purr of an American drawl. 'Beautiful as we
all see it is, and reluctant though you must be to part
with it, Sandra will vow to guard it with her life.' The
said Sandra stepped obediently forward. 'Will you not,
my dear Sandra?' The girl nodded jerkily, eyes like
saucers. 'And return it to you forthwith in one fine, furry
piece, Miss Christhanson...'

Flushing at the utter belittlement of his tone, Jessica
glanced sideways at Teddy, mutely appealing for him to
get her out of here before she disgraced herself and either
gave into a rare burst of bad temper, or broke down and
sobbed her heart out.

Teddy smiled back. To everyone else, it would look
like one of his silly, inane smiles, but Jessica saw the
message in his hooded eyes, and her chin came up. You're
an actress, that look said, so get to work and show the
sarcastic swine what you're really made of!

The coat came off, sliding gracefully from her shoulders. The saucer-eyed Sandra caught it just before the thick, golden fur hit the ground, hugging it to her as though she was ready to carry out her boss's orders to the letter. Jessica stood very still, her slender figure stiff and proud, eyes staring directly into strange golden ones, and it was only the slight quiver to her soft, heart-shaped mouth that hinted at the effort it cost her to do so.

Her dress was a dark red, pure silk shift that moulded to her softly rounded figure to low on her hips, where it flowed gently into a fuller skirt. It was simple and chic; long-sleeved and round-necked. The removal of the coat had revealed the surprising length of her pale blonde hair, falling from a central parting over her shoulders to brush the agitated rise and fall of her breasts.

'Well, I never,' murmured the mocking giant, and his mouth took on the one-sided, upward curve again.

He let his gaze run slowly and explicitly over her, and Jessica stiffened. She had seen that look before—on Joel Blake's hot face just before he launched himself on top of her. Teddy cleared his throat noisily; it was meant as a warning to her as well as a calming reminder that he was there with her.

'A chair for Miss—Christhanson,' the hateful drawl said, and Jessica's pulses began to hammer alarmingly.

Suddenly the quiet room was filled with the sounds of urgency as several people all jumped to obey his command, falling over each other in their eagerness—while she and he remained totally unmoving. Something was happening, something strong and dangerous passing between them, their gazes locked in a kind of battle neither wished to fight nor even acknowledge. This was neither the time, nor the place, nor the person with whom Jessica wished to share that kind of powerful attraction. It scored across wounds too freshly cut by a lesser man than Alec Stedman.

The boy with the bottle-bottom glasses was rolling out a sheet of white paper from a container fixed to the wall;

it was as wide as the platform and he drew it down the wall and across the floor, stepping back while the other young man placed an ornate gilt chair on top of it. And suddenly all that unwanted sexual tension was broken when Alec shifted his eyes from Jessica to look impatiently at the chair.

'Not that one!' he shouted, making everyone jump, including her. 'Hal! Haven't you learned anything in the two years you've been with me?' The one who was placing the chair looked nervously around at the one shouting. 'You don't drown beauty by sitting it on a bloody gilt throne!' The selected chair was waved at scornfully. 'Taste,' he went on bitingly. 'And modesty, man! Leave the rest to lighting—lighting!' he shouted a second time.

'Yes, Alec,' murmured the poor, unfortunate Hal.

'Lighting before props, natural beauty before cosmetics—remember that, Sandra.' He was moving now, that huge frame of his revealing such grace and co-ordination that Jessica stood mesmerised. 'Put the cat down and find something to brush through her hair.' He was still speaking to Sandra. The 'cat' was her coat, which was discarded quickly while the girl scuttled off in search of the commanded brush. 'Touch a bit of colour to her cheeks—unless we can make her blush again—which I doubt. Miss Christhanson doesn't look the type who blushes easily.' A dutiful laugh went up at his attempt at humour.

Jessica didn't laugh; she was too busy clamping down on anger, struggling to maintain her composure, and dealing with the unexpected shaft of attraction she had just experienced for the overbearing giant. You're just overwrought, she told herself impatiently, too receptive to the aggressive male because of Blake.

'Mike! One, two, five spots—soft pink. Three, four and six—a pale violet.' The gilt chair was removed from the platform and being replaced with a plain, straight-backed dining-chair. 'Miss Christhanson,' he turned suddenly on Jessica, 'when you've finished giving your

impression of a marble statue, I would appreciate it if
you would sit on the chair so Sandra can see to your
hair.'

'This way, Miss Christhanson.' The girl's soft voice
came by her left ear, and Jessica blinked, moving like
an automaton to the chair. Alec Stedman was moving
about like a live wire, setting up cameras, snapping out
orders to the boy working the lights so the tints covering
the white-papered area altered subtly.

Through a daze of what, she realised later, was severe
delayed shock, Jessica reacted to the volley of orders
thrown at her from beyond the ring of coloured spotlights. She had suffered her fair share of tedious photo
sessions, even enjoyed a few of them, but this one was
more like a nightmare, curt commands battering her
wilting composure, setting her nerves on edge to the point
where her teeth clenched, her jaw locking—and she
found to her growing horror that she couldn't move,
either.

'Not like that—not like that!' sighed the voice when
she failed to give him the latest pose he required of her.
'I thought you were an actress! Can't you even move
obediently to direction? I want you cool and serene, not
looking like an owl-eyed schoolgirl about to face some
dreaded ordeal!'

She watched, through a strange dizzying haze, as he
ruffled a handful of his tawny hair and pulled at it in
frustration. Then he came over to her, leaping the low
step on to the platform, and loomed over her like some
golden monster from the past.

Sweat was beginning to break out on her skin, she
could feel its clammy coldness trickling down her spine,
glistening on her brow. Her vision was blocked by a hard,
jean-clad thigh, a flat male stomach and the disturbing
sight of taut male skin glowing between the negligently
fastened shirt.

His big hands raked into her hair, allowing the silky
threads to run through his fingers. Jessica stiffened,
stubbornly hanging on to some semblance of self-control.

She would not break down here in front of this man! She would not...

'Texture's wonderful. Who's your hairdresser?'

Jessica told him.

'Clever sod, isn't he? Colour mix is fantastic, never seen a bleach job as good as this. You can hardly tell it's touched up.' His hands were still in her hair, massaging her scalp, raising the nerves of each strand of hair until Jessica thought she was going to scream.

'Teddy,' she said, stiffly, because her jaw wouldn't relax. 'Are you there?'

'Here, sweetie.' She caught his light reply. 'Sitting comfortably, being a good boy, like the man said.'

'Then will you tell this—this blind buffoon to get his hands off me!' Her voice had been rising steadily, and with it her body, coming off the chair in a desperate effort to get away.

'Beg your pardon, lady?' Alec Stedman cut in, sounding as though she had just issued him with the ultimate insult, frowning furiously at her.

'I said, get your hands off me!' she grated. 'Off!' She reached up to shove his hands away, her body shuddering with revulsion. 'God!' she choked, as the panic she should have felt an hour ago, in Joel Blake's suite, hit her with a cloying distress. 'Teddy!' she heard herself call out in a strange, choked voice. Then—nothing—everything seemed to close in on her, darkening in a dizzying swirl of pure anguish.

CHAPTER TWO

'EASY...' Hands as gentle as a nun's came down to cup Jessica's shoulders, the voice soft and soothing on her clamouring senses. 'Easy there.'

She was trembling like a leaf, battling with the desire to faint away altogether, legs like rubber beneath her. Alec Stedman lowered her carefully back into the chair, noting with a frown the look of blind distress on her paste-white face.

'Teddy, whatever your name is,' he went on in that same deep soothing tone, 'what the hell's up with her?'

'Delayed shock,' announced Teddy, and gone was his puerile manner. He was beside her in an instant, squatting down, taking her hands and rubbing them gently. 'Sorry, sweetheart,' he apologised grimly. 'Shouldn't have forced the issue. We can do this another day. Give it a minute, Jess, then I'll take you home.'

'Damn him, Teddy,' she whispered, trying desperately to pull herself together. Her mouth quivered on a painful sob. 'The filthy, perverted b——'

'Is she talking about me?' cut in a confounded Alec Stedman.

'Joel Blake,' Teddy clarified, then cursed when Jessica's trembling doubled. 'Jess, darling,' he murmured, rubbing concernedly on her icy hands. 'Don't torment yourself by even thinking about it! Recall instead how I punched him right on his good side—that should be good for a smile, if nothing else!'

'What the hell are you talking about?' demanded the giant, sounding both irritable and bewildered.

Teddy ignored him. 'He'll have a black eye for days,' he declared with deep satisfaction. 'Imagine the conceited bastard trying to explain that away!'

'Joel Blake *assaulted* her?' Alec Stedman was catching on at last, his big hands leaving her shoulders as he straightened angrily, and Jessica found herself missing his comforting touch the instant it left her.

'On the proverbial casting couch, no less!' sneered Teddy. 'And she's got the bruises to prove it!'

'Sandra!' The golden voice lost its honey. 'Get Aunty Vi to make Miss Christhanson some strong, sweet tea!'

So the old lady *was* someone's aunty! Jessica couldn't help it; she laughed, and went on laughing, finding she couldn't stop; a high-pitched, ear-piercing laughter that ended as abruptly as it had begun when a large, very capable hand made stinging contact with her cheek.

She gulped, stared with wounded eyes at a darkly frowning Alec Stedman, then fell into a silent weeping that took her distress entirely inwards.

Strong arms enfolded her, a warm cheek gentle on her hair, and she felt herself lifted from the chair and cradled against the solid wall of large male chest.

'You hit me!' she accused on a huge sob, then spoiled the rebuke by burying her face in the warm comfort of his throat, her hair spread like fine gossamer over his wide shoulder.

'I had to, I'm sorry.'

'I hate men,' she choked.

'All of them?' he gently mocked, and she felt the ripple of humour run through him. He was carrying her across the studio, the movement of his body disturbing her strangely.

'I feel dirty,' she choked, clinging tighter to him.

'Reaction,' he diagnosed quietly. 'You'll feel much better after a cup of Aunty Vi's tea.'

That made her laugh again, and Alec tensed up a little, thinking she was about to become hysterical again. But this time the laughter died of its own accord, leaving her drained, feeling weary, utterly weary.

They were moving along the 'Rogues' Gallery,' but Jessica kept her face tucked into its warm haven, intensely aware of the male scent of him, the easy swing

of his body as he carried her as if she were nothing but
a featherweight. They passed through a wide archway
into the other wing of the house, and along another more
conventional hallway into a room where she felt herself
being lowered on to something soft. Then a warm cover
was draped over her, and Jessica turned on to her side,
instinctively reaching out to hug a pillow to her, her body
curling up like a child's in search of comfort, the tears
all but dried up now, but the basis for them still clamouring inside her.

She could hear Teddy quietly explaining what had
happened earlier, and Alec's muttered curses as the story
evolved. Then the door was opening and the mood in
the room changed dramatically.

'What the hell are you doing up here?' exploded her
dubious saviour to some poor, unsuspecting victim.

Someone clucked, and Jessica was instantly diverted
when she recognised the familiar sound. A tray rattled
as it was put down, the bed sank close beside her, and
the gentlest, coolest hand came to sooth her heated brow.

'Poor dear,' clucked Aunty Vi, then turned sharply
on the giant. 'What have you done this time, to reduce
the poor creature to this state?'

Jessica could almost see Alec Stedman stiffen at the
curt stricture, even with her eyes tight shut.

'What are *you* doing, climbing those damned stairs?'
came the crackling reply.

'Don't you raise your voice to me, young man!' rebuked an unmoved Aunty Vi. 'I'm not in my dotage yet,
you know!' She returned her attention to Jessica. 'What
did he do to you, dear?' she gently enquired. 'Shout at
you, too, did he?'

'He hit me,' sobbed Jessica, and turned her reddened
cheek up for inspection, enjoying herself.

Aunty Vi's kind eyes went as hard as marbles, while
Alec Stedman glared at Jessica as though she'd gone
completely barmy.

'Alec!' The old lady turned on the big man. 'I'm
ashamed of you—ashamed!' Her cool hand covered

Jessica's abused cheek. 'If it isn't bad enough that you behave like a ogre towards every pretty girl who crosses the threshold—to resort to hitting this poor soul is just going too far—too far!'

'She was hysterical——'

'No wonder, if you hit her!'

'*Before* I hit her, dammit!' snarled Alec.

'He's telling the truth,' Jess put in meekly. 'He—he said I bleached my hair—I got angry, then upset, and he hit m-me.'

'Stop it, Jess,' she heard Teddy murmur, muffling the desire to laugh. 'Good actress you are, pathetic creature you are not.'

'He—he called my coat a—a dead cat! And he accused me of walking around naked beneath it.' Jessica looked limpidly into old eyes crinkling at the corners with slowly dawning amusement.

'Shocking boy!' Aunty Vi condemned, joining in the game. 'Anything else?'

'God almighty!' exploded Alec.

Aunty Vi glared at him, and Jessica hid a satisfied smile. Then those shrewd old eyes were coming back to Jessica. 'Now, will you tell me why my Alec had to slap you?' she asked gently, and instantly the tears returned to the deep blue eyes.

Jessica might have been using her quick wits at Alec Stedman's expense, but only to remove other more intolerable things from her mind. Now they were back with a vengeance, and Teddy stepped quickly forwards.

'Don't, Jess,' he murmured in concern. 'Forget it, it's over. Blake won't get within twenty feet of you again.'

In the end, it was a soft, warm, female bosom Jessica found herself buried in. She heard the old woman shoo the two men out of the room, then gave herself up to the luxury of a good old-fashioned cry to a good old-fashioned aunty, sobbing the whole sorry story out as she did so; and she gained immense comfort from the old lady's occasional mutter of disgust.

'Time for that tea, I think,' Aunty Vi decided when Jessica's sobs had dwindled to the odd sniff. 'Here, blow your nose first.'

A wad of tissues were pushed into her hand, and Jessica dutifully blew while Aunty Vi busied herself with the tea, cups and saucers rattling.

'So,' she passed a brimming cup over and sat down again, 'you came here with all that anger and revulsion bubbling inside you, to take it out on my Alec.'

Jessica's head came up at that, blue eyes flashing. 'He's a conceited, overbearing, arrogant—bully!' she exclaimed mutinously.

'My Alec?' Old eyes turned their censure on Jessica. 'Why——' she patted Jessica's shoulder reproachfully '—he's as gentle as a lamb! Just a great big teddy bear, with a soft-as-butter heart.'

She was like a mother hen defending her chick, and Jessica had to control the desire to laugh. It was so quaint, watching this small, round old lady come out fighting for that big Colossus. She got up, all ruffled feathers and pursed lips, and began tidying the tea tray, then she turned and smiled at Jessica, hostility gone. Aunty Vi obviously believed in saying her piece, then forgetting it. 'You'll want to tidy yourself, no doubt,' she offered thoughtfully. 'Bathroom through that door.' She indicated with a gnarled hand. 'When you feel ready, you'll find Alec and your—friend in the sitting-room. Just turn left through the other door, and it's the second door on the right.'

With that, she hobbled out, leaving Jess alone and feeling not a little foolish now she'd had a chance to think about her behaviour. 'God, Jess!' she sighed out loud. 'When you decide to let go, you hold nothing back!'

She lay back against the pillows, taking in her surroundings for the first time. It was a nice bedroom. Definitely male. Soft beiges and browns, splashed now and then with a rich, warming, rust colour. She was lying beneath a duvet of a soft linen mix of all those colours, chosen by an eye that favoured symmetry in the shape of a large dog-tooth pattern. The same design repeated itself along the full length of one wall and appeared again and again among the soft furnishings.

Nice, decided Jess, and sat up, running her fingers through her untidy hair. I need my bag, she thought, then grimaced when she remembered that it was with her coat somewhere. The bathroom seemed the most logical place to find a comb.

It was only then, as she went to get up, that she realised just how huge the double bed was! It would have to be, she ruefully supposed, conjuring up a vision of the great golden man stretched out on it, hair ruffled in sleep, skin gleaming with the...

A sudden and disturbing rush on her senses brought her off the bed with a jerk, head swimming, eyes glazed with the shock of those unexpected images. Alec Stedman's bedroom, she thought breathlessly. His bed.

'My God, Jess!' she muttered once again, running sweaty palms nervously down her sides when that same powerful stirring that had made itself known in the studio earlier came back in full, assailing force. Then they had been unfavourably confused with her revulsion of Joel Blake, now the two were completely separate, and Jess shook herself sternly, making a quick and agitated escape to the bathroom, berating herself for becoming so stupidly vulnerable to a man she had disliked on sight—hadn't she?

Ten minutes later found her hovering uncertainly outside the door Aunty Vi had directed her to. She still felt a fool—an even bigger one now she had to face those who had witnessed her mortifying loss of composure. She could just make out the low, rumbling sound of male voices coming from the other side of the closed door. It took some doing, but she opened the door...

The two men were sitting talking amicably over what looked like glasses of good brandy. But, on her entrance, the conversation came to an abrupt halt and two heads turned to look searchingly at her.

Controlling the desire to blush like a schoolgirl, she came further into the room, gazing curiously around her so she didn't have to look at those two pairs of perceptive eyes.

He certainly doesn't deny his own tastes, she thought absently, taking in with some surprise the muted greens and soft, classical greys. A lovely Indian rug covered a large part of the polished floor. A wintery sun glinted through the diamond-leaded windows of a deep angular bay, on to the beautiful yew-wood furniture.

'OK, Jess?' It was always a source of amazement to her how Teddy could change from silly twerp to a civilised version of action man in the single blink of an eye. Gone was his rather irritating banter, and in its place that deeper, sharper, more resonant voice that revealed his true dynamic worth. He could manage to look different too, she noted wryly as he came to his feet. He appeared to be taller than the other Teddy. Six feet was not small in anyone's assessment, but Teddy could lose full inches if he decided it was beneficial for him to do so.

'Th-thank you, I feel fine now.' She gave him a wavering smile as he came to lead her to a vacant chair.

Alec Stedman was looking at her narrowly, inspecting, analysing. She was disturbingly aware of the way her senses had reacted to his image back there in his bedroom, and couldn't look at him to save her life. It didn't help that those same feelings came back the instant she'd walked in here. All part of the shock, she weakly excused herself. Great big all-American boys with strange yellow eyes and skin like honeyed gold just weren't her type at all...

'I've arranged with Alec for us to return tomorrow, Jess,' Teddy informed her. 'Just an hour, late afternoon, should do it, and you'll have a chance to...'

'Oh, no, please!' The idea of having to spend nearly twenty-four hours in nervous anticipation of coming back here to face him again appalled her. She might be feeling a fool now, but she knew that by tomorrow she would be cringing every time she recalled today's escapade. 'You know I'm supposed to begin my holiday tomorrow! Can't it wait until I get back?' she appealed. 'Or, better still, can we finish now? I'm fine now, really,' she urged, when both men's expressions were dubious to say the least. 'I don't mind——'

'A month's delay is out of the question,' Teddy told her. 'The magazine who arranged all this need the photographs by the end of this week. Alec has already done them a big favour fitting you in on such short notice.'

The photographs were to accompany an article *Chic* magazine had done on her, due for publication in their next monthly issue. Jessica could see the impossibility of a whole month's delay.

'Then we'll do it now,' she stated firmly.

'No.' Alec came into the discussion at last, sounding smooth but uncompromising. He lifted his hands in a mollifying gesture. 'It matters little to me, Miss Christhanson. I have the time, but I wonder if you're ready to be put through all that just now. After all, it...'

'I'm fine, really,' she once again reassured, then added ruefully, 'I feel a little—silly for my outburst, but otherwise, I'm ready to sit for you.'

'I've let my staff go home,' he told her slowly, watching her face with those strange golden eyes, shrewd and sharp. 'If we work now, then you are going to have to put up with my—overbearing attentions.'

Jess blushed all over again at his cruel reminder of just one of the names she had called him to his aunt. He must have been eavesdropping! she realised gleefully, her own quick sense of humour coming to her rescue as she imagined the big giant doubled over with his ear to the keyhole, and she threw him a provocative glance from beneath her lashes, blue eyes twinkling. 'I could always shout for Aunty Vi if you look like getting out of hand.'

His expression eased into an answering humour, and it was only then that Jessica realised just how serious he had been since she entered the room.

Those large yet beautifully sculpted hands gestured in rueful acquiescence. 'Then let's get started,' he conceded drily, and rose to his incredible height.

It went off smoothly, mainly because Alec put himself out not to upset her. He kept a steady conversation going throughout the whole time, talking in the main to Teddy who, now he had dropped his artificial guise, was deeply interested in the photographer's methods. Alec obligingly gave a verbal narration as he worked, explaining about the importance of lighting, the positioning of the camera and the study, how his initial photographs were taken on a Polaroid film so he could have an instant if not perfect impression of the end product.

The camera clicked, Alec straightened to wait the few seconds or so it took before he could peel off the protective cover from the print and take it over to the light so he could study it closely, golden brows frowning in concentration. Then he was back, altering lights, quietly asking Jessica to move her hand or her chin or some other part of her that didn't quite meet with his approval. His desire for perfection was obvious, the amount of patience he used in achieving it impressive. Click would go the Polaroid again, and off he would go again, studying, criticising in his own mind, coming back, moving something else, until at last he seemed to be satisfied with what the Polaroid print was showing him.

Then he was swapping the Polaroid camera for a more conventional, more complicated kind, and he proceeded to click the shutter at a rate of knots, muttering out gruff commands to her that she obeyed without question.

'Relax a moment,' he said at one point, straightening, focusing on the real live Jessica for the first time in ages, then surprising her with a wide and charming grin. 'I normally have staff to perform this mundane task for me,' he mocked himself as his fingers dealt deftly with the changing of the film roll. For a big man, Jessica noted a trifle breathlessly, he moved with the utmost grace and precision.

From then on he became lost in the art of creating, artistic instinct taking over from conscious mind, and all she and Teddy could do was watch, fascinated by the amount of care and attention he used. And the more he peered at her down his lens, the more conscious of herself she became, the more tinglingly aware of every hair and pore and feature she possessed, until she felt as emotion-ally uptight as she had at the hands of Joel Blake, only in a completely different way. One had been a physical assault on her body, this was more a subtle invasion of her vulnerable inner self.

'Your coat,' Alec said softly, and Jessica blinked once, twice, then blushed when she realised that he must have finished minutes ago and was now standing over her with her coat draped between his spread hands.

He was amused, those yellow eyes telling her he was entirely aware of where she had gone off to in her day-dream, and she was glad to stand up so she could turn her back on him while he helped her into her coat.

The fur fell about her with the warmth and sensuality of a lover's embrace, and she couldn't deny the knowledge that it was this man's touch lingering on her shoulders that gave that fanciful impression. He was standing close behind her, a message so full of sexual motive passing between them that she trembled. Alec let the air come softly from his lungs, and his fingers moved to gently free her hair from the coat's collar, carefully spreading the pale mass about her shoulders, as though reluctant to break contact.

'Th-thank you,' she murmured; her voice was wispy, even to her own ears.

'Have dinner with me,' he invited huskily, ignoring Teddy's interested observation.

'I don't think...'

'Please,' he urged softly, and Jessica was no match against the low throb of appeal in his voice.

'I—all right,' she agreed.

He turned her then to face him, his strange eyes warm as they studied the light flush in her cheeks, the silver arc of her shyly lowered lashes, the slight quivering of her vulnerable mouth.

'I'll pick you up at eight,' he said.

Jessica nodded mutely, and at last found the strength to move away from him, walking blindly from the platform and over to where Teddy waited in rueful silence.

They were at the door when his voice stalled them. 'Jess?' he called softly.

'Yes?' She didn't turn to look at him, didn't have the courage.

'Have a nice long bath,' he said huskily. 'I don't want you confusing me with that swine Blake again.'

She nodded slowly, her long hair brushing against the thick fur of her coat. 'I don't think there's any chance of that,' she told him, and heard his breath leave him on a satisfied sigh.

CHAPTER THREE

HER doorbell rang promptly at eight o'clock. Jessica turned to view herself in the long mirror in her bedroom. The coffee-coloured, drop-waisted dress suited her slender figure, the colour complementing the smooth creaminess of her skin. Strapless, it clung to the soft swell of her breasts, skimming loosely over her waist and hugging her hips, the crêpe de Chine material moving softly with her body. She had washed her hair, and dried it with the aid of heated rollers to give the ends some bounce, then drawn up the two side wings and fastened them away from her face with a casualness that left fine, wispy bits brushing her cheeks and brow.

The long soak in the bath had been entirely successful: she was now over her unhappy experience with Joel Blake, and the whole nasty ordeal had been shoved to the very back of her mind. Which left room only for Alec.

She looked honestly into her own eyes, and saw written there what she knew he would see when he looked at her. Attraction—strong, undeniable attraction, more potent because of its essence of surprise. She felt alive and sensually female, her skin tingling with an excited anticipation that put soft colour in her cheeks, made her mouth turn upwards slightly at the corners, as if it couldn't help but display that inner glow she was feeling.

The doorbell went again and she moved away from the mirror, making no attempt to school her features. At the front door she paused, feeling as breathless as any teenager about to go out on her first real date. She opened the door.

He was still the giant, was her first dizzy thought, the awesome and dominating Colossus, dressed to do battle on her mortal senses. His dinner-jacket was white and beautifully cut, his shirt a soft oyster shade of pink that took her by surprise, his bow-tie white and silk. He wore black raw silk trousers that hugged his flat hips and accentuated the dangerous power in those muscled thighs of his. He was leaning casually against the doorframe, a hand lost in his trouser pocket, and his expression was—mocking.

'I thought, for a minute there, you were going to stand me up.' Those lion eyes ran lazily over her. 'I'm glad you didn't,' he added softly, and his look said why.

Jess took wry note of the butterflies that took up residence in her stomach. 'It never occurred to me to stand you up,' she told him softly.

'Thank you, for that,' replied Alec, and the tingling increased, because he was looking at her so seriously, with such deep intensity. 'Ready?' he enquired without bothering to invite himself in. A lopsided smile took away the serious look. 'You look delicious enough to eat, but I'll restrict myself to conventional food if you'll just get your wrap before I give in to—other temptations, and decide to eat à la Christhanson instead of à la carte!'

Jessica laughed, appreciating his dry sense of humour, and his gaze slid down to fix on to her soft mouth.

'The wrap,' he reminded huskily.

'The wrap,' Jessica repeated breathlessly, and turned in a silly fluster to go and get her white fur wrap, wondering dazedly why he was affecting her so badly, so soon. She wasn't usually given to instant attraction. In actual fact, she wasn't known to behave this way at all!

His car was long, expensive and powerful, the rich cream colour a reflection of his very distinctive taste for light and space. He courteously saw her seated on the cream leather passenger seat, squatting down beside her to personally fasten the seat-belt around her.

His face was close to hers and she couldn't seem to stop herself turning that small inch which would bring their gazes level. His fingers stilled, strange eyes darkening to a liquid topaz. We're going to be lovers soon, that look said. I know, her own replied, and the reflex jerk of a muscle in his jaw was answered by her own shaky sigh.

He got up swiftly, closing the car door and striding around the car to climb in beside her, sexual tension so potent between them that it held them in thrall.

'Where in America do you come from?' Jessica asked him in an attempt to break the tension.

He turned a white-toothed grin on her, long hands caressing the steering wheel with all the sensitivity that was evident in the man. 'New Yorker,' he announced mockingly, 'born and bred.'

'So what is a "born and bred New Yorker" doing living and working in London?'

He gave a casual shrug, glancing briefly over his shoulder before easing the car into the stream of traffic. 'Faces,' he said when the manoeuvre was complete, then went on to explain, 'My forte, if I have to give what I do best a name, is in catching on film those character-istics in a woman which show her at her most beautiful, without the aid of disguising cosmetics or clever camera filters. You can study any of my portraits and compare them favourably with the unadorned real thing.' He shrugged, as if to lightly dismiss his natural gift, but Jessica was sure he didn't treat it lightly at all. 'I stand by the philosophy that no woman is unattractive. They all have something beautiful in them, be it an inner glow of a lovely nature, or maybe one special physical feature. All it needs is finding and using to its best ad-vantage... look at Aunty Vi, for instance,' he went on. 'She is sixty-nine years old, and her face shows every line of pain she has suffered over the last ten years.'

'Arthritis?' Jessica inserted sadly.

Alec nodded. 'But her eyes sparkle with a natural mis-chief no amount of pain can smother, and her smile can light a darkened room. If I were to photograph Aunty Vi, I would crack a joke that was ever so slightly *risqué* to make those eyes twinkle and that smile come out, and no one would even notice the pain lines, the age lines, the bend in her nose where she broke it once in a fall from a horse.'

'But every country, every city has its share of beautiful and ugly faces,' Jessica argued. 'So I can't understand what all that has to do with your preferring to work here rather than——'

'But you've missed the point,' he drily cut in. 'As I said, I don't believe in ugliness.' Jessica was lost, and showed it in the look she levelled on him. 'What some American women have done,' he went on patiently, 'the ones who can afford me to photograph them, anyway,' he added with a grin that was all self-conceit, 'they have become so obsessed with achieving their idea of perfection that they've ruined the natural beauty mother nature gifted them with! Cosmetic surgery, dental surgery, *bone* surgery!' he said scornfully. 'They even go so far as to have themselves restructured to look like a current film star! Just try to imagine—hundreds of Victoria Principals walking about the place, or Diana Rosses in the case of the lovely black American!' He made a sound of disgust. 'They leave me nothing to work with, it's like photographing waxwork dummies. But what they *don't* see, as they throw away fortunes to achieve their ideal face, is that they lose their own individuality in the process, leaving them with a rather benign beauty that excites no real man.'

'Phew!' Jessica breathed, surprised by the passion he had said all that with. 'That is some dangerous philosophy, likely to cause you trouble if it's ever made public.'

'I make no secret of the way I think,' he defended rather haughtily, raising those golden brows at her. 'Now, the women here have yet to surrender to the ''plastic'' bait. Except for the very few, the faces are in general honest to themselves... I expected yours to be a plastic face,' he wryly threw in, glancing briefly at her to see how she took that observation. Jess looked suitably insulted, and he grinned wickedly before returning his attention to his driving. 'I saw your last film, and you looked so damned surface-perfect that I decided it had to be a case of an expert plastic job.'

'Thank you,' she muttered, ruffled. 'Here I am, twenty-three years old, and already trying desperately to hide my age with——'

'Ah, but there is my point. You see, you only *look* eighteen! And I, in my regrettable cynicism, decided that you were just too perfect to be true! So it had to be a classic case of artificial aids.'

'If there was a compliment in there somewhere,' she drawled, 'I'm afraid I missed it.'

'Sorry, Jess,' he murmured, barely hiding his amusement at her pique.

'Sorry?' she scoffed. 'The man calmly informs me that he thought me an old hag struggling to look half her age—and he expects to placate me with a simple, "Sorry, Jess!"'

'Oh, not an old hag,' he protested, pulling the car to a stop in a small side street and shutting off the engine before turning to face her. It was then she saw the amusement, the mockery, the little yellow devils dancing in his eyes. 'Never a hag,' he repeated softly, humour fading into something else as they gazed at each other. 'And never old.' He reached out to run a finger down her cheek. 'You're one of the lucky ones,' he told her gravely. 'You'll always look young, beautiful, infinitely desirable.'

His gaze ran possessively over her face, ardently appreciative of her milk-white complexion, the fine, silver brows and long, curving lashes. Her eyes, a clear and startling blue, revealed to him a level of awareness that made him sigh softly as his thumb ran lightly over her full lower lip.

'Perfect,' he murmured. 'The most perfect face I've ever had the privilege to look upon.'

What about the beautiful Tracy? she found herself peevishly thinking. His wife had been—and still was, by all accounts—incredibly beautiful.

'Do me a small favour, Jessica,' he requested seriously. 'Don't ever be tempted to change a single feature for the sake of "fame".'

He made the word 'fame' sound like a shocking sin. 'I'll make a bargain with you,' she offered, her ever-present sense of humour coming to the fore. 'I'll give you that promise, if you'll promise me...' Her gaze ran consideringly over his own rock-hard and too, too attractive face, holding the moment full of delicious anticipation with the ease of a good actress, and she could see by the way his eyes narrowed that he was mentally going over his own feature faults, waiting for her to make some stinging criticism. '...if you'll promise me never to call me "lady" in that oh, so degrading way you did this afternoon!'

Alec looked first confused, then thoroughly rueful because she had caught him out completely. He leaned over to place his lips against hers in a brief but tantalising kiss. 'You have that promise—*lady*.' And he gave the word an entirely new and euphoric meaning, making those resident butterflies flutter.

The restaurant was small, intimate, exclusive and French. They argued pleasantly over the menu, made mocking remarks about each other's choice, and generally behaved like a pair of light-hearted fools, Jess mused as they lingered over coffee. He had gone out of his way to charm, and she had been more than receptive.

'Tell me about Blake,' Alec said suddenly.

Jessica glanced sharply at him, then looked down quickly, studying the way her fingers played idly with her coffee spoon. 'I still can't believe that I fell for it!' she sighed. 'I hadn't even wanted to read for the part. Teddy talked me into it. We went along to Joel Blake's hotel suite—nothing unusual in that in my business, a lot of visiting directors audition that way... He was all charm, all graciousness. He gave me a copy of the script and left me alone to glance through the scene he wished me to read while he took Teddy through to another room—to get his opinion on a piece of porcelain he had just acquired. Teddy is a collector of fine porcelain,' she broke off to explain, 'and noted as an authority. Neither I nor Teddy thought it odd that he split us up in this way. Joel came back alone, leaving Teddy, he told me, drooling enviously at the piece of Meissen. It was only when we were settled down on his couch and were reading the script that he suddenly pounced.' She shuddered at the memory. 'I fought him off and he got nasty, throwing all kinds of threats at me about ruining my career and all that rubbish.' Her mouth took on a bitter line. It was plain to see that that kind of threat held no weight with Jessica. 'He'd got my dress half off by the time I had the sense to call for Teddy. He shot into the room— Teddy isn't what he appears to be, you know,' she thought it fair to add.

'I know,' he said quietly, and he did. Teddy fooled many, but not Alec, not even from the beginning, when he'd been at his most frivolous.

'Teddy dragged the lecherous old swine off me, punched him in the face, then spat so many insults at him that I couldn't begin to list them. Teddy also wields some fearful power in our profession, and Joel Blake is aware of that. He was visibly scared stiff.' An odd smile touched her mouth, and Alec looked enquiringly at her. 'Teddy picked me up,' she continued with that smile still there, 'dusted me off—as the saying goes—and bundled me out of the suite. He then disappeared back inside again. I heard the sound of breaking china, then Teddy was outside with me again and frogmarching me towards the lifts.' The smile widened and became very smug. 'He'd smashed the porcelain,' she confided. 'Said to me "Damned awful thing, anyway."' She exactly matched Teddy's affected drawl. '"Had no right to wear the Meissen mark!" He must have been angry to do that, though,' she added pensively. 'Teddy would rather cut off his right hand than damage a piece of precious porcelain normally. I must find something special to replace it.'

'But the Meissen didn't belong to Teddy!' Alec pointed out.

'No.' Her expression was quite serious, her affection for the fashion-plated Teddy as clear as day. 'But he'll feel its loss—here——' she touched her heart with all the drama of an actress '—and by now will probably be cursing his own impulsiveness.'

'So,' Alec prompted gently, 'you came directly on to your appointment with me, feeling less like being photographed than a man with no face at all——'

'And you promptly made me feel worse by verbally attacking me as soon as you saw me!' she finished for him drily. 'That remark about my being nude hit a raw nerve, I can tell you. I don't know why I didn't slap your face.'

He sat back, grinning, looking purely the wicked giant. 'Have you ever played a nude scene?' He was being deliberately provocative. Jessica's blue gaze widened.

'Definitely not!' she hotly denied.

She'd stopped fiddling with the coffee spoon, and was now fingering the fine stem of her wineglass instead. Alec was watching her with a possessive look in his eyes that hadn't wavered all evening. She could feel them on her now, burning into her, stinging her pulses into life, diverting her, making her want to——

She glanced up and glinted a wicked smile at him. 'I was once *expected* to do a nude scene in a film,' she admitted impishly.

'Which film?' he immediately demanded, frowning at her, those golden brows almost touching over the long, arrogant nose. 'I thought I'd seen all your films, but I don't remember any nude scenes.'

'All three of them?' She mocked her own success. Jessica was a theatre actress first and foremost. Her short career in feature films had been a mistake as far as she was concerned, one she hoped to rectify soon. 'John Crowther's *Downfall of a Legend*,' she informed him in answer to his question. 'John organised a closed set, gave the order for action, and I was supposed to walk naked out of the bathroom and over to the bed, where my co-star waited in full bronzed splendour beneath a black silk sheet strategically draped over his thighs. I was the siren, the direct cause of his downfall, so I had to appear lethal, totally irresistible.'

'But I remember that scene,' Alec cut in. 'You came out of the bathroom dressed in the sexiest underwear I've ever seen!'

Jessica nodded ruefully. 'I couldn't do it, you see, couldn't walk on to the set with no clothes on to save my life! So I went all out to seduce with every bit of sexual allure I had in me, knowing I would only have one chance to convince John that a highly charged sex scene could be created just as successfully with clothes as without. It worked.' She smiled her relief. 'John let me off, and the scene stood as I'd played it.'

'I know,' he murmured huskily. 'It was the only time I ever wished for an action replay in a full-length feature film... You were wonderful.' His eyes darkened disturbingly, and Jessica saw his thoughts turn inwards, remembering, reliving that particular scene in the film...

She had sauntered into the bedroom wearing a pure white silk camisole and cami-knickers edged in soft lace, her skin like cream, body in smooth, sensual motion, hair loose around her shoulders—a shimmering mass of pale blonde. She'd reached the side of the bed, and the camera had cut to the impassioned face of her handsome co-star. There had been no words, no seductive background music, just the silence and the darkness and the soft pool of light spilling over his face, the highly charged atmosphere had been left to the two actors to create. A hand had reached out to stroke her thigh, and the contrasting impact of tanned male skin on pale female flesh had set the pulses pounding. The hand had moved, the camera following its slow and sensual progress up her thigh until it had slipped beneath the loose lace hem of the cami-knickers—then it had cut to Jessica's face, showing her head thrown back in erotic delirium, eyes closed, mouth slightly parted, hair brushing sensually against her naked back, and the atmosphere shot to a pulsing, throat-drying pitch which left the viewer breathless. It had been enough, Jessica wryly recalled now. John Crowther's brilliance was in his ability to know when to call a halt on a scene and leave the rest to the imagination. The hero was hooked, and about to begin his fall from legendary fame, everyone who saw the scene knew that.

'Beautiful, seductive—a siren,' Alec murmured throatily. 'Yet still managing to maintain that air of exclusivity I see as an inherent part of you, the real person.'

'I was wearing the most modest pair of passion-killers beneath those sexy silk ones,' Jessica announced, and giggled irresistibly when he jumped, his rapt gaze losing out to utter disappointment.

'That was cruel,' he accused painfully. 'You've just spoiled my most favoured fantasy scene I like to take to bed with me at night.'

Jessica leaned over to give his hand a consoling pat. 'Your ardour needed cooling,' she mocked.

'Bitch,' he said.

'Hmm,' agreed Jess, smiling.

'Can I see you again?' They were sitting in his car outside her flat.

Jessica was genuinely sorry. 'I'm away for the next month,' she told him. 'A holiday—long overdue.'

Alec looked as though she'd hit him, and her blue eyes softened into understanding; she was feeling a bit the same herself.

'Teddy did make mention of it this afternoon,' she reminded him.

He nodded, fingers tapping on the steering wheel, eyes averted, glaring blankly out of the windscreen. 'Where—where are you going?' He tried to sound careless, but only managed to sound gruff and sulky.

Jessica smiled sadly. 'My plans are—transient,' she evaded. Well, she excused the half-lie, they were. She wasn't sure to which part of Greece she would be going until Stavros called her in the morning to confirm her flight booking. But the reason for the evasion was sitting, big and golden, right next to her. She was just a little afraid of the strength and speed with which she had become involved with him. 'I've worked non-stop for five years—ever since I left drama school—and I'm tired,' she explained gently, because she didn't want to hurt him, leave him believing she was just making excuses. 'Both mentally and physically drained, even a little disenchanted with the direction my career is taking. I need time to find myself again, decide what I'm going to do next. If I stay here in London, there will be— pressures brought upon me to make decisions I'm not ready to make.' The length of her explanation alone told Alec how important it was to her that he understand— just as she understood his impatience. A month was a long time when feelings were running as high as theirs were.

'The Joel Blake film?' He turned to look at her.

Jess shuddered. 'No!' she denied. 'No, I have to decide between doing more film work—as my darling twenty- per-cent Teddy wishes me to do,' she said wryly, 'or going back into theatre as I want to do.'

'And I want you to stay here with me,' Alec put in huskily, then added ruefully, 'More pressure.'

'Nice pressure, though.' She reached out to touch his hand, and he moved his from the steering wheel to catch her fingers, drawing them to his lips. 'And very tempting.'

His eyes darkened, and he moved closer to her, leaning across the narrow gap between their seats so his mouth was a mere breath away from her own. 'We could,' he mused suggestively, 'go up to your apartment and discuss this further—in comfort.'

'We could,' she whispered, watching that beautiful mouth with a craving he couldn't miss. 'But...'

'But you don't think things would turn out quite like that if we did?' he quizzed, mocking himself as well as her.

'Things are moving a trifle fast for me, Alec.'

'Frightening, isn't it?'

'Very,' she breathed, and on a soft sigh closed the gap between their mouths.

Electricity formed a melding between them as instant as it was unnerving. His mouth was warm and persuasive, his tongue rubbing against her lips, urging them to part for him, and she responded eagerly, as hungry as he to know the moist intimacy of unconstraint. His hand slipped to her nape, holding her face up to his, and she gave an involuntary shiver, for the kiss was infinitely more disturbing than any other she had experienced, making her aware of every nuance of their embrace, of the muscled pressure of his body against her own slenderness, the stimulating scent of him, the overwhelming sense of helplessness in being wanted by this golden giant of a man.

Jess arched up to meet the weight of his body as it crushed down on hers, and her hands came out to touch him, running inside his open jacket so she could press him to her. She could feel, at last, the taut strength of his body with fingers which trembled over heated skin beneath the sensual smoothness of silk. Alec responded with a muffled groan, deepening the kiss with a hunger that had her reeling.

It took the harsh blast of a car horn to break them shakily apart. Alec remained hunched over her, eyes like burning topaz as they gazed into her love-glazed ones, chests heaving as slowly they struggled for recovery.

'All right?' Alec asked huskily.

Jessica nodded mutely; she couldn't have spoken if she'd tried. She had never, ever experienced anything like the feelings so fiercely aroused in her with that one single kiss.

'Like a runaway train with no driver.' He tried for humour, but only managed to sound shaken.

'Or a driver who has lost control of his train,' she amended shakily.

Alec rested his brow against hers, his breathing ruled by the unsteady rhythm of his heart. 'I want to touch you all over,' he said gruffly. 'I've wanted to from the moment you removed your coat in the studio today. I wanted to span your waist with my hands and hold your body against mine, so that you can feel how much I want you, too! I want to lie down with you, touch you, feel you, know you!'

'Sex,' she labelled it huskily, and he smiled as he pulled away from her a little, his fingertips lingering to brush lightly over her face, learning, enjoying, needing.

'Delay your holiday,' he urged softly.

Jessica shook her head, denying her own desires as much as his.

'I may try to come back earlier,' she compromised. 'But I am committed to go for a month, and it will hurt those who are expecting me if I cut short my stay.'

'A man?' he snapped, jerking away from her.

Jessica felt cold suddenly. 'Family,' she drawled, and Alec had the grace to look uncomfortable.

'Sorry.'

'You don't particularly sound it,' she said, then sighed, because this was going all wrong and she didn't want the evening to finish on a bad note, especially when she would be away so long. 'Give me three weeks, Alec,' she appealed quietly. 'Three weeks!' She placed her fingers over his mouth when he went to protest. 'Too much, too soon,' she whispered. 'I'm not used to—committing myself to a relationship so impulsively.'

'So you admit we have something going for us,' he drawled a little bitterly. 'And more than just a passing thing!'

Jessica's laugh was self-derisive. 'I've admitted that to myself from the moment you picked me up in your arms this afternoon. Give me my holiday, Alec,' she asked in a cool, less impassioned voice. 'If I can, I'll come back sooner, but I just can't see me daring to leave before three weeks. Give me three weeks and I'll call you as soon as I get back, hmm?'

'Call me?' he sneered, hands back to tapping the steering wheel. He glanced angrily at her. 'Then what?'

Jessica felt a sharp rise of irritation, and had to bite down on the cutting remark that leaped to her lips. He had no right to think he could demand so much from her on the strength of one date! He had no right to . . .

'Then we take it slowly,' she decided coolly, then spoiled the effect by muttering, 'I think.'

Alec humphed out a scornful laugh. 'I should have taken you up to your apartment, taken you to bed and loved you senseless, then we wouldn't be sitting here, having this stupid discussion!'

'I wouldn't have let you make love to me!' she replied indignantly.

'Of course you would, Jess.' His confidence stung. 'Your eyes tell me you would, your body tells me, your hands told me when they touched me—and don't you dare deny any of it, Jessica,' he added gratingly. 'Or I may just get angry!'

'I think you're already that,' she muttered, then sighed in irritation. 'I can't believe you actually expected me to let you into my bed on just one date!' she breathed angrily. 'What kind of impression do I give of myself, for God's sake, if you can . . .'

'A sweet, very exclusive, very selective impression,' Alec groaned contritely, pulling her back into his arms and holding her tightly. 'I'm just disappointed,' he excused his ill humour. 'Because you're going away, and I'd planned on seeing you tomorrow night, and the night after that, and——' his mouth lifted into a lopsided smile '—and maybe the night after that, to take you home to my bed.'

'Then you can begin your—campaign when I get back from my holiday,' suggested Jessica on a softer note.

Alec pushed her away from him, looking grimly into her eyes. Then he kissed her, briefly and hard, on her surprised lips. 'To remind you of that promise,' he said. 'Now, get out of my car, there's a dear, before I ruin my reputation as a sophisticated lover and take you here and now, in full view of anyone who wants to watch!'

CHAPTER FOUR

WAS there anything more mystically moving than viewing the jagged Greek coastline from an unimpaired twenty-eight-thousand feet up in the air? Jessica decided not as she peered eagerly through the porthole of the British Airways 737 she was travelling on, sighing out loud at the glory of a pure blue Aegean Sea framing the ruggedness of a beautiful and historical land. They passed over islands, some just tiny dots in the wide expanse of glittering blue, others huge bulks of land with names as famous as their ancient gods.

She felt a little godlike herself, Jessica thought dreamily, looking down from the heavens just as those mythical gods must have done all those thousands of years ago. Zeus, Apollo and Aphrodite, discussing the Fates over wine and fresh, juicy figs. No matter how many times she made this trip to Greece, the magic never dulled, the air of mystery and excitement could still hold her enthralled.

The plane began to lose height, steadily dropping down over the cluster of small islands, banking around the tip of Turkey and continuing to bank as they swung in a wide arc towards the enchanting island of Rhodes, bathing in a late February sun.

It seemed mere minutes before they were over the island and low enough to pick out smaller details like the ancient Rodian Castle dominating the town, Mandraki Harbour where the Colossus—dedicated to Helios the sun god—once stood, one hundred feet high and forged in bronze, his powerful legs spanning the harbour mouth, protecting the people from hostile invasion. He guarded no longer, that huge golden giant, brought tumbling down by an earthquake centuries ago.

A strange gleam entered Jessica's dreamy eyes, and repeated itself in the soft curve of her mouth. The Colossus might have fallen prey to an earthquake, but he hadn't disappeared for ever, just slumbered for a few thousand years, then returned in mortal form. Alec Stedman form.

She could see the the bay of Ixia now, where modern hotels hugged the rolling hillside, and the fine shingle beach washed gently by a lazy Aegean. It was clear of sun worshippers at this time of year, but within a month or so it would be alive with holiday-makers, when the Greek summer really began.

The banking plane began levelling out, and Jessica barely had a chance to note they were about to make their final approach into Rhodes Airport before they were rushing along on a level with the land. Then, with a soft bump, they were landing, and her thoughts shifted from the fanciful to the realistic when a new excitement gripped her, that of knowing she was mere yards away from the people she loved most in the world.

'Jess!' The cry went up even before she'd come through passport control. She looked up eagerly, searching for the familiar pale blonde head of her sister, and saw her beaming an excited smile that would be exactly mirrored on Jessica's own face.

They went into each other's arms, laughing and crying in the same excited breath. It was easy to see the relationship of the two women; only sisters could look so much alike.

'Mama and Thia Jessica are crying, Papa!' chimed a small, indignant voice. 'Why are they crying when they should be happy?'

Jessica turned within her sister's embrace to look fondly at her nephew, who was gripping his adored papa's hand and looking like a miniature replica of him. Stavros Kirilakis stood tall and distinguished, his dark, attractive face showing a lazy mockery.

'Ah—my son,' sighed Stavros in answer to his son's contemptuous enquiry. 'Women are such capricious creatures, they cry when they should laugh and laugh when they should cry. It is a trial, I know.' He shrugged in the typical Greek way. 'But we males must allow them their moments of sentiment.'

Stavros turned his laughing gaze on Jessica then, and his smile broadened, his arms opening wide in welcome. 'Jessica, my dear,' he murmured, and she went willingly into his embrace.

'Still disregarding the rules, Stavros?' she quizzed when she'd come up for air, taunting the fact that he had arrogantly brought his family to meet her in what was a restricted part of the airport.

He was not in the least perturbed. 'See how I risk imprisonment to welcome you to my home?'

'You're nothing but an arrogant devil!' she scolded laughingly, then turned her attention to the last member of her welcoming committee, her four-year-old nephew.

'Yannis!' she greeted softly, dropping to her knees in front of his sturdy little frame.

He was eyeing her dubiously. Yannis was as proud and arrogant as his papa, and he didn't like weeping females. His adored papa had accepted Jessica without hesitation, so, in his baby eyes, he should do the same, but he was afraid she might start weeping all over him. Jessica knew all this without having it explained to her.

'I like the T-shirt,' she said, in a blatant attempt to ingratiate herself with him, making sure she laughed to show him she had no intention of crying again.

Yannis put a plump brown hand to his tummy, where the haughty face of Paddington Bear looked out at her from beneath his floppy hat. Jessica had sent it to the little boy as a gift for his birthday, along with the genuine stuffed Paddington Bear.

'Papa likes it, too.' Papa's opinion was of paramount importance to the little man. If Jessica was agreeing with his dear papa, then perhaps she wasn't so bad.

An idea brought a wicked gleam to Jessica's blue eyes. 'Then I'll buy him a T-shirt just like yours for his birthday!' she declared.

'God forbid!' spluttered a deep voice.

'And a Paddington Bear hat,' she continued gleefully, 'because I think he's too old for a stuffed bear now, don't you think?'

The little face beamed in delighted agreement. Stavros choked on a muffled curse, and Jessica received her prize in a strangling hug from the little boy, while Helen's pretty laugh sprinkled them all.

The Kirilakis villa nestled into the hillside of a small private bay on the quieter side of the island, near Lindos. Stavros brought them home by sea, sailing his motor yacht around the island and into the bay, so that Jessica could see the family home from this beautiful vantage point. The setting was idyllic, the house a delight, and it was at that moment, with her sister's family around her and her heart full of love for them, that she decided she would not cut her holiday short for Alec or anyone else.

Her resolve lasted just over two weeks.

Instead of considering her career, she found herself daydreaming over a pair of strange yellow eyes, which were filled with a passion that set her pulses racing. He appeared before her when she was building sand-castles for Yannis, helping Helen set the dinner-table, when she should have been listening to what Stavros was saying. She found herself wondering just how Alec would look, stripped to a pair of brief swimming trunks, rising out of the warm Mediterranean Sea after a strenuous swim, tawny hair slick to his head, water gushing off his golden frame. She saw him in the middle of the night, when he came to intrude on her dreams. She saw him everywhere, and in the end, on a burst of frustration, she packed her bags and pleaded with her brother-in-law to get her on the next flight home to England, going red and flustered when she had to explain her reasons for wanting to leave them prematurely, and then having to put up with Stavros's teasing for a whole day until her flight arrived.

'Take care, Jess. Don't get that soft little heart of yours broken,' was all Helen said when she kissed her goodbye at the airport. Wise Helen could still remember what it felt like to be in the state Jessica was in.

Take care, she thought heavily as the plane took off. How does one take care when your whole being urges you to be reckless?

She arrived at her flat three days earlier than Alec was expecting her back, and the first thing she did, once she'd dumped her luggage, was call him.

She got Aunty Vi.

They chatted quite easily for a few minutes once Jessica had explained who she was, then she asked to speak to Alec. 'Is he there?' Her nerves were already fluttering in anticipation. What if he'd got over her? What if he didn't want to speak...

'Causing minor wars in his studio,' his aunt complained. 'He's been like that for over two weeks—— You wouldn't have anything to do with his bad mood, would you?' enquired the shrewd old lady.

'Oh, I do hope so!' laughed Jessica. 'Do you think he'll mind my disturbing him while he's working?'

'I think you've already done that,' laughed Aunty Vi. 'Hang on a minute, while I buzz through to him.'

'Jess, where the hell are you?' Alec's deep American drawl bellowed down the phone at her.

'Why, at my flat, of course,' she replied innocently. 'I did promise to call...'

'Three weeks, you said,' he all but accused her.

'Oh, well,' Jessica pouted, and it sounded in her mocking tone, 'if you're going to grumble over the odd day so—I'll call again next week.'

She went very quiet, as though intending to put down the phone, smiling to herself because she could tell she had thrown him totally.

'Jess!' he grated harshly.

'Yes?' she said softly, and gained delicious satisfaction from his long, impatient sigh of relief.

'Why are you back so soon? I mean, what did you call me for . . . I mean . . .' He was floundering! she noted with wicked triumph. The great and sophisticated Alec Stedman was knocked off balance!

'I was calling to invite you to dinner,' she cut in carelessly. 'But you sound so unapproachable that perhaps it isn't . . .'

'Shut up,' he muttered.

'Yes, Alec,' she replied meekly.

'Dinner,' he said huskily, and the telephone wire began to sizzle. It was back, that wild and wonderful zing of attraction.

'Please.'

'At your place, or out?'

'Out, I'm afraid,' she told him. 'I've only just got back home and my cupboards are bare, so to speak.'

'Don't use that word,' he protested mournfully. 'Bare, I mean,' he clarified, then laughed ruefully at himself. 'Why are you home early, Jess?'

She pondered that soft-voiced question. 'How big is your ego?' she threw back drily.

'Not half as big as some parts——'

'Alec!' she cried, interrupting him before he made her blush. She heard his soft laugh, and knew he considered her paid back for her teasing of him.

'The dinner I accept, the place I choose, and the bill I pick up,' he went on with more of his usual arrogance. 'That ego you spoke of won't allow a lady to pay for the pleasure of my company.'

'I'm not arguing, am I?' Jessica was female enough not to need a women's lib façade to prop her up.

'I'll be there for seven, and—Jess,' he murmured huskily, 'wear your hair up for me, hmm?'

'Why?' she said, frowning.

'So I can enjoy the pleasure of loosening it later,' he whispered.

'Arrogant——'

The line went dead. The last sound she'd heard had been Alec's warm laughter, like velvet on her excited nerves.

Alec stabbed impatiently on her doorbell right on time, and Jess was already waiting on the other side to answer it.

She was wearing white tonight, a soft, filmy, lace affair with full long sleeves and slightly padded shoulders. The wrap-over design of the dress fastened at her waist with two diamond-studded clips, and formed a deep, dramatic slash down the front of the top, so the material brushed invitingly against the smooth swell of her breasts, the flowing skirt swishing as she walked. She had coiled her hair on the crown of her head as requested. Diamonds glittered in her ears, at her throat and around her wrist. She looked beautiful, a very sophisticated, very expensive lady, and Alec took his time taking in every single detail with those yellow eyes narrowed and intense.

'I wish I had my camera with me,' he murmured gruffly, and lifted his lids to look deeply into her anxious eyes. 'Beautiful, Jess, absolutely beautiful.'

She swallowed tensely. 'Thank you,' she whispered, then mentally shook herself to smile wryly at him. 'You don't look so bad yourself!'

He was in black tonight, conventional dinner-suit black, with a plain white silk shirt and black bow-tie. His tawny hair shone like silk, and his skin still wore that golden colour she had come to think of as his alone.

'Lethal,' he said about her.

'Dangerous,' she described him.

Alec lifted a hand to her cheek, his fingers deliciously cool against her heated skin, flushed a little beneath his warm gaze. 'Why did you come back early?' he asked her softly.

'The train was going so fast that I couldn't get off.'

Those yellow eyes flared. 'And did you want to get off?'

Her mouth quivered on an unsteady "no".

Alec growled something in his throat, then was getting rid of the unwanted space between them by gathering her into his arms and kissing her deeply, restoring her faith in their mutual attraction, making her feel that at last she had come home.

Jessica was still shaken by the speed and intensity with which their feelings had erupted when they reached their destination a little later. Alec drove with his attention only half on the road; his eyes kept flicking restlessly over her, burning where they touched. Conversation came in short, brusque bursts, his lean face taut, stiffly controlled, until Jess was visibly strung up and anxious. She had expected a strong reaction when they met again; if her weeks away had done little else, they had forced her to accept the power of their attraction for one another, but this—this total breaking down of the senses—frightened her a little.

The tension between them heightened as they entered the club, and his hand on her waist bit a little in his desire to keep her as close to his side as possible. She felt small and rather fragile next to him, and she found it impossible to utter a single word to ease the gnawing sexual awareness throbbing between them. Her hair brushed lightly against the crook of his shoulder as they walked, her cheek close enough to his body for it to tingle with a delicate flush of awareness.

The waiter held a seat for Jessica to sit down, but Alec stalled her, his grip tightening on her waist. 'Champagne,' he ordered curtly, then dismissed the waiter by turning his attention on Jessica. 'Dance with me,' he muttered, and she glanced nervously up into his face at the curt demand in his tone—then quivered when she saw rigid tension grabbing at his face muscles.

Without waiting for her to reply, Alec took her purse from her and threw it down on the table, then led her to the dance-floor. His arms came around her, holding her close, moving them around the tiny dance-floor to the soft, slow music. They weren't the only ones dancing, but they were the only ones doing so with this level of

intimacy so early in the evening, and Jessica became em-
barrassingly aware of the curious and sometimes amused
glances they were receiving from the others present in
the club.

'I couldn't sit down, not yet,' he said tensely. One of
his hands splayed between her shoulders, the other lay
low on her spine, his body curved to all but envelop
hers, his mouth brushing her ear. 'I needed to hold you—
hold you!' he grated in a harsh whisper.

'Please stop it, Alec,' Jessica pleaded shakily. 'People
are looking.'

'Ignore them.' He pulled her closer, bringing her hard
against his thighs, so she could feel the appalling tension
in him. 'God——' he choked. 'I shouldn't have brought
you here, not tonight, not in that dress. I should have
taken you to my bed, instead!'

Jessica sucked in an angry breath. He was behaving
shockingly. Her cheeks were stinging with embarrassment, eyes lowered so no one watching them could
read just how much his attitude was upsetting her. With
deliberate intention, she curled her fingers into his arm,
digging in with her nails until he jerked in surprise.

'Stop it!' she hissed a second time.

At least he had the grace to gather himself then, body
stiffening, a small gap appearing between them.

'I'm behaving like a——'

'Don't say it!' she cut in sharply. 'I know exactly how
you're behaving!' They were talking in hushed voices,
Jessica's hot face hidden in the shadow of his wide chest.
She had never felt so embarrassed in all her life...nor
so atrociously receptive. Her heart was hammering like
a machine gun, her limbs trembling.

'Sorry,' he muttered. Jessica didn't dare look at his
face, she had a feeling Alec was blushing a little, too.
'Let's go back to the table——'

'No!' God, had he lost all his mind? 'Just—just
behave, that's all,' she whispered angrily. 'We'll sit down
when the music ends, as normal people would do.'

'Yes, Jess. Sorry, Jess.'

Was he mocking her? Her anger moved up another notch, and she braved a swift glance at his face. He was dancing so circumspectly now, and looking so much like a stiff-necked idiot, that she couldn't help but giggle.

'Poor Alec!' she mocked in sympathy. 'You sound like Teddy: "Yes, Jess. No, Jess. Three bags full, Jess."'

'Thanks!' he muttered in disgust. He looked down into her ruefully teasing face, and smiled naturally at last. 'Do you have this effect on every man who comes close to you?' he murmured. 'Turn them into babbling fools, with their brains sunk as low as their loins...'

She giggled again, and the tension between them began to ease. Jess put a finger into the deep cleft in his chin, languidly watching the way his jaw clenched at her touch. 'I like this,' she murmured softly. 'It speaks of strength and character.'

Alec caught her hand and dropped a brief kiss on her fingertips, placing her hand palm-flat against his chest, holding it there beneath his own. His fingers squeezed once, then relaxed, and Jessica knew that it was his way of apologising for his behaviour. She gave her forgiveness with a warm smile.

'No sign of either quality evident tonight,' he quipped. 'No strength, no character, no...'

'You're sounding like Teddy again.'

'Can we sit down now, Jess?' he requested painfully. 'I think I would feel a lot more comfortable with the solid width of the table between us.'

'Of course we can sit down,' she said gently, her heart squeezing for this big giant who was in so much turmoil because of her.

She slipped an arm around his waist, leaning lovingly against him as they went back to the table, uncaring now of the curious looks they were receiving. Jessica was aware that both their faces were probably recognisable to some, but she didn't care, didn't care about anything any more but being with him.

'Just how tall are you?' she asked curiously as he guided her to her chair. She didn't think herself short, but Alec seemed to dwarf her, even in her high-heeled shoes.

'Six feet four inches, ma'am,' he stated in his best New Yorker accent, bowing formally before sitting down himself, hitching his large frame on to the seat in a way that said how inconvenient his size could be sometimes, especially in a confined space such as this. 'One hundred and eighty-nine pounds,' he went on mockingly. 'I have all my own teeth.' He showed them to her with a wide, false smile. 'And I passed my last physical, A1 fit.'

'Age—you forgot your age!' she laughed.

'Thirty-four years old, ma'am!' he offered promptly, mischief twinkling in his lion eyes. 'Graduated with honours. Married once, divorced once, and——' He stopped abruptly, and Jessica almost groaned as all the sparkle seemed to drain out of him. 'But you probably know all about that. Shall we order now?' he finished grimly.

Alec behaved impeccably for the rest of the evening, putting himself out to charm and amuse. They ate, drank champagne and even danced some more, but as soon as they climbed back into his car at the end of the evening the tension came back with a vengeance, spiced with an unwillingness on both sides to approach the subject most prominent on their minds.

Jess was very much aware that it had been she who had set the guidelines they were supposed to follow from this point on. But that had been before she went away, and she was ready to admit she had made all that suspect by coming back early from her holiday.

'Have you come to any blinding conclusions about your career while you were away?' he broke into the strained silence to ask.

Jessica shook her head. 'Not yet, but I still have some of my month's holiday time left to decide.' In actual fact, she hadn't been able to give her career more than a cursory thought. Alec had filled her mind.

'Why a month?' he enquired. 'Why the specific deadline?'

'A film part,' she explained. 'I have an option to star in John Crowther's next film. It would mean a six- or seven-month stay in California. John gave me a month to decide, because he won't begin auditioning proper until then.'

'I see,' murmured Alec, and Jessica could tell that he *did* see. This sudden and unexpected attraction she had for him had only added to her dilemma, because she knew that if it was to be allowed to grow into its full potential then there was a chance that, when the time came, she wouldn't want to leave London—and have him working half-way across the world from her. 'You think I'm going to put pressure to bear on your decision, don't you?' He glanced shrewdly at her. 'But I won't. I would be a fool if I tried to influence you on something as important as this. In reverse, I would resent anyone trying to do that to me.'

He *was* influencing her, anyway, Jessica thought wryly. Just being here with him was an influence in itself.

'The alternative is a play,' she went on, making no comment on his remark. 'Due to begin rehearsals next month, in the West End.' She paused as he braked at a red traffic light, his indicator flashing his intention to turn right towards her flat, and her hand went jerkily to his thigh, feeling that hard muscle clench in reaction at the unexpected contact.

'Alec,' she whispered breathlessly, 'don't take me home.'

That was all. 'Don't take me home.' And the silence inside the car was harrowing. Alec sat stiffly beside her, his fingers gripping the steering wheel, eyes frowning blackly at the red traffic light.

'Where?' he bit out.

'Your house,' she whispered, and the friction holding them shot out of control.

CHAPTER FIVE

THE traffic lights changed to green. The car shot forwards, fooling everyone behind them by going straight on instead of turning right, and Alec exploded with crude profanity.

'Why did you *do* that?' he grated harshly.

'Switch off your indicator.'

'What?'

'Your indicator,' she repeated unsteadily. The air in the car was thick with an angry violence. 'Switch it off, you're confusing the other road users.'

His fist knocked the indicator lever, his expression like a volcano about to erupt. 'Damned stupid way to tell a man...' he was muttering, jerking the car through the gears as if needing to vent all that pent-up emotion on something solid.

'I fancied a cup of tea with your Aunty Vi!' Jessica said in a hopeless attempt at lightness. Inwardly, she was as surprised as he that she had said what she had. She was further surprised at Alec's angry reaction.

He exploded with another volley of expletives, and Jessica retaliated fiercely. 'Swear once more, Alec, and I'll call this whole thing off! I'm——'

'Sorry!' he grated.

'No, you're not!'

'No, I'm not!' he agreed tightly and threw her a vicious glance. 'Have you any idea what it's been doing to me all evening? Sitting there, going crazy with wanting you, and knowing that I have to behave myself, *woo* you——' he made it sound like a sin, and Jessica stiffened with offence '—deliver you back to your damned— *sorry*—your door with just a chaste kiss and a smile for my trouble!'

He was driving the car down the main street with a lack of concentration that was in danger of having them pulled up by the police. Jessica's hands gripped the seat, her heartbeats pounding in her ears as she watched in fascinated horror as he swerved in and out of the traffic with bare inches sparing precious car paintwork.

'Have you no idea what that dress has been doing to me?' he went on furiously. 'That your nipples show dark and dusky against the lace, that every time you move a certain way I get tormenting glimpses of soft, creamy flesh? That I can see more than is decent, right now?'

Jessica flinched, her hand going up to her bosom to cover the deep V in her dress on a mortified gasp.

'Now she covers up!' he scorned cruelly. 'After half the male population of London has had its fill!'

'I think I hate you,' she whispered painfully, immeasurably hurt by his harsh censure. He was exaggerating, taking the shock of her impulsive announcement out on her, venting some of that built-up sexual tension without caring what it did to her. 'I've—I've changed my mind. Take my home. I don't want to be with you, after all. I don't——' She had to pause to swallow on the great lump of tears blocking her throat. Alec cursed quietly beneath his breath and ground the car through yet another ill-fated gear. 'I don't w-want a great over-sexed gorilla in my arms. I don't w-want y-you any m-more!'

'Easy, honey.' All at once it was Alec being gentle, soothing her with his golden voice, the only hint that he'd been angry at all was in the slight hoarseness in his tone. 'Come on.' His hand came out to grip hers, squeezing them where they lay, mangling each other on her lap. 'I'm sorry... I keep saying that, don't I?' he mocked himself ruefully. 'But I am—sorry. Don't cry, sweetheart. I'll feel the true heel if you cry.'

'You *are* a heel,' she sniffed.

'And the rest,' he agreed huskily. His eyes were on her, Jessica could feel them flicking anxiously from her to the road then back again. His driving had calmed, along with his temper. On a heavy sigh, he moved his arm around her trembling shoulders. 'Come here,' he said softly. 'Come on, put your head on Alec's shoulder and I'll promise to be the good all-American boy my mother reared me to be.'

Jess let him pull her closer to him, sniffing to show her reluctance, then surrendered to his gentle pressure and let her head rest against him. It was such a broad shoulder, so warm and firm and...

'Brute,' she muttered, just to let him know he wasn't forgiven yet.

'Anything you say, Jess,' conceded Alec heavily. 'I've just made the momentous decision not to argue with you ever again... I don't like it when I make you cry, honey,' he told her softly. 'It makes me want to cry, too.'

Mollified, Jessica snuggled closer, watching him drive efficiently, one-handed. 'I missed you while I was away,' she told him.

'Keep quiet now, Jess,' he ordered grimly. 'It just isn't safe for us to talk in potentially dangerous situations. Let me see if I can manage to get us both to my house in two whole pieces, hmm?'

Jessica pouted. 'I just wanted you to know, that's all.'

'Jess...'

'I'm trying!' she flared all over again. 'Do you think I'm not as knocked off balance as you are?' Her head came off his shoulder, and she returned to a rigid position in her own seat, cheeks flushed and eyes sparkling. 'That two grown and supposedly sophisticated people can behave like this over something so—elementary as sex...'

'There's nothing elementary in what we're experiencing, Jess.' It was Alec's turn to be calm, hers to explode. He huffed out a soft laugh. 'I'm only afraid that if we don't get to my place soon there's going to be one hell of a nuclear fall-out in this car, and we'll both end up being blown sky-high on it.'

'*I'm not used to this!*' she choked, becoming agitated.

'So you keep telling me!' he sighed, and the derision was back in his voice.

Alec spun the car wheel so violently that Jessica was thrown against his shoulder. It didn't feel as comfortable when hit at speed, and she rubbed at her cheek, peering out of the window to see why he had taken such a drastic action.

They were driving through the high wooden gates to his home. Alec guided the car around to the rear of the house, the headlights shining on a pair of garage doors, one of which began swinging smoothly upwards as they approached. Alec drove inside, bringing the car to a stop and shutting off the engine before sitting back in his seat.

'It's the truth,' she dropped mulishly into the ensuing silence.

'I know,' he answered quietly. It was dark in the garage. She could barely make out his features, but could easily sense his weary mood. 'Your reputation is famously unimpeachable.'

Jess winced as if stung. 'While yours is—notorious.'

She sensed him turn his head to look at her. 'Don't hold it against me, Jess, because I can't offer you the same.' He sounded very grim. 'Just trust me, when I tell you that this is different. This,' he sighed, 'I'm not used to, either.'

Strangely, she believed him.

'Can we get inside the house without alerting your aunt?' she asked unsteadily. 'I don't think I could cope with the necessary social niceties tonight.'

'Of course we can,' he assured her deeply, and at last reached out to touch her.

Jessica let out a shaky breath, taking that big hand in hers so she could hold it against her cheek. Alec responded by turning her face to his and kissing her softly, without any of the passion that rang furiously inside both of them.

They climbed out of the car with no more said, meeting at the garage door, arms going around each other as

they walked towards the house. Alec let them in through
a rear door and led the way up a narrow flight of stairs,
Jess trailing behind him with her hand clasped warmly
in his. They reached the first floor, then went through
another door which brought them directly into a super-
efficient kitchen.

'The house is split into four sections,' he answered the
unspoken curiosity in her gaze. 'The whole house belonged to Aunty Vi originally. She really is my aunt,' he
added on a wry grin. 'Well, near as damn it, anyway.
My mother's stepsister. She inherited the house from her
natural father, and lived here alone for twenty years
before I arrived on the scene. That was...' he paused
to make a brief calculation, moving past Jessica to fill
the coffee percolator '...five years ago now. I'd come
over from New York, and was on the look-out for some
decent property I could use as a studio. I came to visit
Aunty Vi—a duty visit,' he added drily, pulling a face
that said he didn't like admitting that. 'She is my only
living relative, and I felt I should meet her once before...
Anyway...' he shrugged off the uncomfortable feelings
bothering him and at the same time motioned Jessica to
a chair at the scrubbed pine table, removing his jacket
and bow-tie and loosening his collar '...I arrived to find
a ''For Sale'' sign stuck in the hedge outside. Met this
endearing old lady with the stupidest dog I've ever seen,
both of them mourning the prospective loss of the only
home they'd ever known, and trying bravely not to show
it. It had just got too much for her, you see.' He was
moving around the kitchen with the same deftness she
remembered him using in his studio. It was a pleasure
to watch him, listen to his rich golden tones, study the
lithe movement of hard muscle beneath his thin shirt,
his size so at odds with his natural grace.

'So she was selling up, intending to move into what
you English call Sheltered Housing.' His grimace showed
what he thought of that idea. 'It was right there and
then, as I listened to her valiantly trying to instil enthusi-
asm in her voice, that I came up with this idea.' He ges-

tured with a spoon to the kitchen, including the rest of
his apartment. 'I suggested that I buy the house from
her and, to save an old lady's pride, I convinced her that
I needed looking after—protecting from those lascivious
females who flock after my body,' he added on a grin.
'To cut short a long story——' and to skim over his own
beautifully generous nature in concerning himself with
an old lady's problems, Jessica made mental note
'—Aunty Vi has one half of the ground floor as a self-
contained flat. The other half makes up the more formal
reception rooms I sometimes have a necessity to use if
I entertain—except for the dining-room,' he paused to
point out, an odd smile touching his mouth. 'Aunty Vi
insists on cooking dinner for me. One square meal a day!'
He mimicked his aunt's bossy manner. 'She insists that
a big man like me has to have one square meal inside
him a day and has decided it is her duty to provide it.
I eat it in the dining-room downstairs because I won't
have her climbing the stairs to serve me here. Up here I
have my studio, darkrooms, office and so on, which takes
up one half—and this,' he motioned again to the
apartment in general, bringing two steaming mugs of
coffee over to the table and putting them down before
hooking out a chair with his foot and sitting down beside
her, dwarfing the poor spindle-backed chair, which
creaked beneath his added weight, 'is my own private
apartment. I have my own entrance, so I can come and
go as I please. Then there's the main front door you
came in by last time you came here. That one Aunty Vi
reigns supreme over. She's nosy, you see,' he confided
on a glinting smile, and Jessica thought, what was it
Aunty Vi had called him? Nothing but a great big teddy
bear. She was right, Jess acknowledged now. 'She likes
to know what's going on up in my studio, she likes to
see who's coming and going, thinks she keeps tabs on
me that way. But she gets frightened when she's on her
own at night, so she bolts the front door when everyone's gone home for the day. She has Samson to keep
her company, and he's a good guard dog, believe it or

not.' Jessica visualised the big dog lying across the foot of the stairs, and smiled. Samson looked too lazy to 'woof' most of the time. 'Then there is the intercom system I had installed, which connects her to any part of the house if she feels she needs me.'

'And you can't get more "sheltered" than that,' Jessica noted gently.

He sat back in his chair and it protested all over again. Jessica wondered absently if he had to replace them often. They surely couldn't take that kind of treatment indefinitely!

Then her mind pulled a rotten trick on her and had her wondering what it would feel like to have all of that weight pressing down on top of *her*, and her senses began to shift again, fanning alive the passion they had both managed to subdue for a short while.

'She was burgled once,' Alec was saying, and Jessica blinked, realising with a jolt that he must have been speaking to her and she hadn't heard a word. She reached for the cream jug in a desperate attempt to appear at ease, then wished she hadn't when her hand shook so much that Alec had to take it from her, quite gently, his topaz eyes telling her he knew exactly what was happening to her.

'Hence her decision to sell—and the arthritic hip, of course.' He continued to tell his tale, pouring some cream into her cup for her as he did so, but his voice had a huskier quality to it now. 'All in all, it was my good fortune that I came along when I did. This place is well situated to central London, where most of my clients live, and I have both working and living accommodation in the one deal. Aunty Vi and I get on famously. She has her old cronies around several times a week and, if I can, I go down and charm them all a bit. She likes that,' he said with a smile. 'She puffs up as proud as any mother hen—and, by return, she doesn't interfere with whatever I do up here.'

'No scolding on your rakish ways?' Jessica teased.

'No scolding,' he confirmed softly.

Jessica sipped at her coffee, but she didn't want it. Alec sipped at his, but she knew he didn't want any, either. His gaze was warm on her, and a prickling began at her nerve-roots, thrilling her because she knew how much he liked looking at her.

'Jess——'

She jumped when he said her name, then laughed a trifle nervously, putting down her cup before she dropped it. 'I'm frightened,' she admitted ruefully. He was sitting very close, close enough to reach out and touch her. She threw a quick glance at him from beneath her lashes; he looked very serious. 'Crazy, isn't it?' she mocked herself shakily.

'Then we won't go any further than this,' he said, so very gently that it sent a wave of tenderness through her. 'We'll drink our coffee, then I'll take you home... I want you to be sure, Jess,' he said solemnly. 'Sure of me, and what you want from me, because this thing between us isn't going to diminish with one single coming together. It's too strong for that—much, much too strong.'

'I know,' she agreed huskily. 'But that isn't what I meant.' And oddly, that wasn't what was bothering her; it had earlier in the evening, but not now, not now they were alone like this, together. 'I think it's you I'm afraid of.' She gave a funny laugh.

'Me?' Golden brows rose questioningly, then lowered again when some sort of comprehension hit him. Jess glanced sideways at him, embarrassed. 'Jess, are you trying to tell me——?'

'No,' she quickly denied what she knew then he was thinking, a blush colouring her cheeks. 'No, I'm not—virginal.' She made it quite ruefully clear.

There was a tense pause while Alec's mind turned over slowly. Then the back of his hand came out to brush her warm cheek. 'I'm not Goliath, you know,' he teased her gently.

'No?' she quizzed, and knew then, with a further heating of her cheeks, that she had given herself away.

Alec let out a choked laugh. It wasn't amused, or mocking. Just—choked. 'I don't believe this!' he breathed, 'Jess——' His hand moved to her nape, forcing her to turn and face him. His expression was stunned, warm and tender, but stunned. 'Jess... Loving bridges all kinds of physical differences. When the mutual bond of passion, desire, care and consideration are used...'

'Sure they do.' She tried to sound careless, but only sounded terribly gauche.

Alec studied her narrowly for a moment. 'How—experienced are you, Jess?'

'Not very,' she admitted, with a bitter twist to her soft mouth.

'God!' He sighed. 'Not very,' he repeated to himself. 'I wonder what that means.'

Another sigh had him reaching out to her and pulling her gently but firmly on to his lap. 'Feel that?' he questioned gruffly, holding the flat of her hand against his chest, where his heart hammered against her palm. 'Remember that kiss we shared in the car before you went away? You weren't afraid of me then,' he stated knowingly. 'Your heartbeats matched mine then, and you wanted me—only me. The only uncertainties you had then were to do with other, more practical, problems.' Topaz eyes searched her confused face. 'When the need is that strong, and the chemicals are working, and the time and place are right, it can only be perfect for us—surely you must know that?'

She nodded shyly. Of course she knew. She was no silly young girl struggling with her first encounter with a man! It was just—just... She gave up trying to put words to what was bothering her, and looked instead into the disturbing depths of Alec's eyes.

His lap was firm beneath her, his body a beautifully honed rock for her to maroon herself on if she only had the courage. As if understanding her confusion, Alec let her see the passion and uncertainty he, too, was feeling. Her mouth parted, the pink tip of her tongue flicking nervously over her lips. Alec watched the movement with a taut stillness, eyes fixed on that moist tongue-tip. And, as he had said, the chemicals began to flow, her body coming alive as they stared at each other, her mind slowly blotting out the doubts, the fears, to leave only him, and her, and the magic they knew was theirs to reach out and take whenever they were ready.

'Kiss me,' she said, and it was an oddly broken little plea.

She felt his body stir beneath her, his chest heaving on an unsteady breath. 'Dammit, Jess,' he murmured, and crushed her to him, taking her lips with all the hunger his sensual nature could throw at her.

His hand slid inside her dress, moulding one silken shoulder, the other hand on her face, fingers trembling as they stroked so lightly over her skin that she wanted to sigh at his gentleness. Her mouth parted, taking his with it, and on a sudden frenzy of need their tongues met and clung. Deep inside her, she felt her own response dart in rhythm with his tongue; up and along her body it went, like a flame out of control, enveloping her until she felt scorched, alive to every minute part of him. She arched closer to him, breasts throbbing with an aching pain that was sheer pleasure.

Alec muttered something against her mouth. Her palms were rubbing at his shoulder, moving the thin silk against his hot skin, her fingers digging into thick, hard muscle, their tremours impossible to separate as that kiss deepened into a heated exchange of desire. He moved forwards, his huge frame trapping her against the table, tipping her backwards until she lay cushioned against the hardness of the wood table by his arm. She heard the scraping sound of crockery being shoved aside, knew a sense of indescribable weakness drain all the strength from her limbs, then Alec was leaning over her, his free hand urgently brushing the top of her dress away from her breasts.

She felt a rush of cool air hit her fevered skin, then his hand closed over one aching breast, kneading, moulding, his thumb working on its pulsing tip until she felt an agony of constraint build inside her.

'Alec——' she breathed, and he moved jerkily away from her, sitting back for the moment it took him to catch his breath, eyes burning over her in one swift grazing of her exposed flesh. Then he was scooping her up into his arms and coming to his feet, that big and beautiful body trembling with the effort it cost him not to take her there and then in the graceless clutter of the kitchen.

It was that quick and that urgent, this all-consuming effect they had on one another. Jessica clung to him as he carried her through to his bedroom, her mouth moist on his throat, her kisses hot and fervent. She was almost out of control when he laid her gently on his bed and arched over her to issue another of those long and clinging kisses.

'How do I get you out of this lovely thing?' he said gruffly, tugging at her dress.

'It fastens at the waist,' she told him breathlessly, and watched the mesmeric power of topaz move down her body to search out the two diamond clasps at her waist. He had them undone in a second, then was parting the material, searing freshly exposed skin with his hot gaze and witnessing triumphantly the way her muscles moved in a quivering response.

'So white, so soft, so smooth,' he murmured. 'You're beautiful, Jess, beautiful.'

The dress discarded carelessly to the floor, Alec bent to kiss her hard on her parted lips, then cruelly broke the connection, refusing to listen to her broken protest as he turned his attention to her hair, carefully removing the pins, his touch so gentle on her scalp that she shivered. He took his time, eyes narrowed in deep concentration as he fanned the soft, silken mass out across his pillow.

'This is how I've dreamed of seeing you,' he told her with husky intensity.

He moved away, and Jessica opened her eyes to watch him begin removing his own clothes. The only light in the room was a frosted moon shining in through the uncovered window. It slid like platinum on gold across his naked skin, and Jessica shook on a soft sigh of appreciation for that large chest liberally covered with fine threads of tawny hair.

His fingers went to the buckle at his waist, then paused. 'Close your eyes,' he commanded softly.

Jessica shook her head. 'I'm not afraid, Alec,' she assured him on a breathy whisper that ran over his skin like hot silk. 'Not anymore. I want you, I want to look at you. I want to know and feel and *be* you!'

That wonderful chest moved on a great intake of air, then settled slowly back again as he quickly removed the last barrier of clothing from his body. Alec was well aware of the response his physique aroused in women. It even evoked a small sense of power and pride in him that they showed a certain awe of him. But not Jessica. He felt a new and dire need never to frighten Jessica. She looked so infinitely vulnerable, lying there, so fragile and pure, so utterly precious to him.

She was watching him, all eyes, languid, liquid eyes. The moon slid lazily over her pale body, where only the flimsiest scrap of silk prevented him taking full visual delight in her. Her hair fanned the pillow like a silver aureole for her delicate beauty, and a surge of desire rushed through his veins, tensing his muscles, holding him still as he stared down at her unblemished beauty.

Like a god, Jessica thought breathlessly, like the proud Colossus. Male perfection personified.

When he came down beside her, she sighed softly, going into his arms as if she belonged there. Alec held her close, letting her take her time to enjoy the ecstasy of their two bodies closely entwined.

His hands splayed her slender hips, fingers gently urging the final barrier away with such sensual grace that she arched for him, aiding him, and Alec caught her to him, holding her so that she would know how desperately he wanted her. His mouth sought hers, and the rush began again, swinging them upwards, tossing them high on a rolling wave of sensuality.

His mouth on her breast was warm and moist. Jessica pushed instinctively against this point of aching contact. A hand was caressing her stomach, gliding over its smooth flatness, seeking out in deeper degrees of intimacy her most sensitive areas, arousing her to a pitch where she found she could not distinguish one pleasure point from another.

'My silver lady,' he whispered, just as his fingers slid into the soft cluster of pale curls and at last made contact with her aching centre. She was ready for him, pulsing and arching to a rhythm he set for her, and carefully, before his own delirium of need spiralled him out of control, Alec moved to cover her body.

He was hard and strong, his body bathed in a fine sheen of sweat that Jessica sipped at with her tongue. Her hands moved on his majestic frame, caressing, pleasing him with her touch. They were barely breathing, taking in air in soft, gasping breaths, each one dragging them deeper, holding them lost in the beauty of each other. She could feel the pressure begin to build inside, and turned her mouth to his shoulder, biting sensuously on the sweat-smooth skin.

'Alec,' she whispered desperately. His caresses were throwing her into a mindless panic. 'Alec——' Her fingers dug fiercely into him.

'Ssh,' he soothed, brushing an unsteady hand over her hair, and looking deeply into her anxious eyes. 'It's all right—ssh——' he hushed again.

His eyes closed, golden lashes lowering slowly over topaz, the hot glow of desire in his cheeks, and on a telling shudder he eased himself into her, taking his time, teeth clenched in an effort to make the moment perfect for her. Her arms came around him, her body opening to welcome him with all the sensual promise of her nature, and all desire to hold back deserted him as they moved together in perfect harmony, each powerful thrust of his body drawing him deeper and deeper inside her until Jessica knew the full force of the power he wielded as he lifted her, triumphantly tossing her into a place beyond bearing.

He felt her go, felt her breathing still, her body tense, then explode off the edge into mindless pleasure, and it was then and only then that he followed her, letting go of the last threads of his control and surging up to join her until, on a strangled cry, they became lost, as wave after wave of swirling pleasure became their prize.

CHAPTER SIX

IT HAD been quick, too quick: the weeks of frustration culminating into that one explosive union. And it needed little insight to know how deeply shaken Jessica had been by the force with which they had ignited each other. It could have been a brutal experience if Alec hadn't managed to maintain some semblance of control.

Jessica was lying very still against him, her body curled close to his, legs entangled, cheek resting on his slowly steadying chest.

'OK?' he asked softly.

She nodded, her hair brushing his chin.

She wasn't asleep, but then he'd known that by the way her long lashes moved like silk against his skin. Alec frowned, sensing her deep introspection.

'Is it always like that?' she asked him quietly.

He stopped breathing for a moment, then heaved in a deep breath, his head coming down to rest on the top of hers.

'No,' he answered, 'not always.'

She heard the note of puzzlement in his tone, as he moved far enough to snatch up the trailing sheet and bring it billowing over them, covering their cooling bodies.

'Jess, you were no novice to——'

'It's never happened like that for me before,' she confided softly.

Alec shifted, dipping his chin in an effort to see her face, read her expression, but she wasn't letting him, her cheek was pressed down against his chest, and Alec laughed softly, touched by her shyness.

'It was pretty special for me, too, baby,' he told her, his accent thickening in a way Jessica had noticed it did at the expense of his emotions. He stroked his fingers through her hair, absently smoothing the fine strands away from her face. 'I was sure it would be,' he went on. 'But not quite so—unequivocal. Jess?' A sudden thought shook his confidence. 'You did enjoy—I mean, I didn't——'

'I've only known one other lover before you,' she interrupted shyly.

'I don't want to know, Jess,' he cut in stiffly, hard jaw clenching. 'I'm not into swapping experiences. So...'

'No.' She moved suddenly, coming up on an arm to look at him, laying a hand over his mouth to stop him talking. 'No, this is important to me. Please listen?'

Jessica saw the anger in his eyes for what it was—a defence against what he thought was a threat to his ego. Topaz shot with gold flickered, then the anger was fading to be replaced with a resentful compliance, and she settled down again, removing her hand from his mouth to run her fingers absently through the sweat-dampened whorls of golden chest hair.

Now she had his attention, she wished she hadn't asked for it. How could she explain, after what they had just shared, what was troubling her mind?

'I was twenty years old and as naïve as they come— still am, I'm coming to realise,' she added, with a sardonic touch unusual for her. 'He was a fellow actor, handsome, full of his own conceit.' Her soft mouth twisted, and Alec watched the play of emotions chase each other across her face, beginning at last to understand. 'Selfish to the last, I now see.'

'Are you trying to tell me that you—you never...' He floundered, and she cut in quickly to save him, because she knew herself how difficult this subject was to discuss out loud.

'I'm not quite that naïve!' she derided. 'And his ego wouldn't allow him to leave me—untouched, by his loving. You understand?' He frowned, and Jessica sighed, wishing she hadn't started this. 'It doesn't matter, forget it,' she murmured foolishly. 'It was a stupid conversation, anyway.'

'Hold on a minute.' Alec pushed a hand beneath her chin to make her look at him. 'What is it you're getting at, Jess? Are you trying to tell me that you never...?'

'Not like that, no,' she admitted on a shaky little laugh that held no humour.

'Then—how——?'

'He—he...' She wriggled in discomfort. It was no good, she couldn't say it out loud and, on a rush of embarrassment, turned her head to whisper quickly in his ear.

'Well, I'll be...' he murmured, and Jessica glared at him for looking so stupidly pleased for some reason. 'How long were you with him?'

'Six months. We lived together for most of that time, but it wasn't a successful arrangement.'

'I'm not surprised,' he drawled.

'I decided to get out. He wasn't that concerned.' She shrugged fatalistically. 'He said he was bored with me, anyway, that—that I wasn't—passionate enough.'

She could still hear the echo of his contemptuous voice as she prepared to leave him. 'All that cool, clean beauty isn't just skin-deep, is it, Jess?' he'd sneered. 'It goes right through. You're a bore, Jess. You don't know how to spark a man to life—you don't even want to!' The Silver Madonna, he'd called her, and it had been no compliment.

'And now you know differently,' Alec murmured into the heavy silence. 'Come here.' He pulled her to lie across his body, cradling her like a baby to his chest. 'So you've spent the last three years avoiding any heavy relationships because of what that—swine said to you.' Once he caught on, Alec was very quick to perceive the bits left unsaid. 'So, why make me the exception to your rule?'

She smiled at that. 'Why did you make me an exception to *your* infamous rule?' she threw back lightly, snuggling up against him. 'I was led to believe that you never, ever made a play for any of your models.'

'You're not a model,' he pointed out.

'But I am from that world you're famous for despising. That fickle, flighty world of glamour and overgrown egos. Why, Alec?'

'Fate?' he offered, hoping to divert her by stroking a finger down her sensitive spine. Jessica shook him off, refusing his answer. 'An irresistible temptation to my senses?'

'Closer,' she allowed.

'OK.' He sighed. 'I give in, what made us both make momentous exceptions to our own rules?'

'This,' she whispered, and covered his mouth with her own, eliciting a kiss that moved the earth beneath them, yet wrought no sexual tension. It was a kiss of tender betrayal, pointing towards, but not quite stating the word 'love', though they both knew it was there, lingering in the background, waiting for the right moment to reveal itself in its full, incontestable glory.

Alec was shaken, but in hiding when they emerged from that embrace. But Jessica didn't mind his elusiveness. She knew, understood. Words didn't need to be spoken in confirmation. They were already there, floating in the air around them. Love was the reason they had both cast aside their rules. It was the reason Jessica had gone away, to come to terms with the blinding, stunning shock of falling head over heels in love with a man she had only just met.

If to love Alec meant risking him discovering her own sexual inadequacies, then she'd had to take it. The risk had paid off, for in surrendering to him, she had been set free from all those useless inhibitions. Alec had been set free also, though he wasn't ready to acknowledge that yet. His wife had hurt him deeply, and naturally he didn't want to experience that pain again, so he had put his deeper feelings into cold storage, carefully selecting his female partners so they posed no threat to him. But when Jessica came along he couldn't ignore what was taking place between them, and in that alone admitted—unconsciously at least—that what they had was something too special to turn away from because your deeper emotions were under threat once again. Their coming together had sealed a bond forged nearly a month ago on sight. The rest would follow at a slower pace, but it would come.

Jessica yawned, curling up against him. They hadn't spoken a word to each other since the kiss, and his frown, Jessica knew, was a mark of his thoughts. She pressed her mouth to his warm throat, then closed her eyes, drifting immediately into an easy sleep.

They made love again during the night. And when Alec lay deep inside her, his big body slick with the sweat of love, pressing her down into the soft bed, she nothing but a boneless insignificance in the turgid power of their spinning senses, he kissed her, giving back what she had given him with that earlier kiss. No words, just a silent commitment that went beyond words.

They slept and awoke still entwined, close in spirit as well as body.

Breakfast brought with it silly nonsensicals—jokes, teasing, laughter and touching—always the physical expression to strengthen the bond.

'I've decided to audition for the play,' she announced over toast and coffee.

He made no remark, but it was only as his facial muscles slowly relaxed that Jessica understood how much he had wanted her to say that.

She took a bite at her toast, and thick, melting butter dripped down her chin. A long finger snaked out to scoop away the creamy butter, and Alec licked his prize with a deliberate sexual relish.

'Can't have my best dress-shirt spoiled by grease marks,' he scolded, eyes twinkling.

While he sat there with that big golden chest boldly unshirted, she was wearing the shirt he had discarded the night before. It reached right down to her knees and almost swamped her. But it smelled of him, and she hugged herself in it, revelling in the intimacy. However, it brought a thought that made her frown, even while her gaze was rueful.

'I'll have to sneak out of here before your staff arrive and catch me *in flagrante delicto*, so to speak.'

'I like you just where you are,' Alec told her arrogantly. 'Why worry what others may think?'

'God, what will Aunty Vi say?' she exclaimed, visualising the old woman's disapproval even now.

'She'll scold you for ruining my virtue!' Alec promptly predicted, and received a blow to his chin for his trouble. That started a play fight that ended up with them sprawled across the kitchen floor, Alec's shirt no longer a decent cover of Jessica's undeniable charms, his naked chest pressing her down on the hard floor so she had to shriek in protest.

There they lay, Alec on top of Jessica, grinning stupidly at each other—when the unexpected opening of the kitchen door sent them through several stages of shocked reaction.

'Oh!' gasped Sandra, blinking down at them. Her employer's huge golden frame was almost completely obliterating a mortified Jessica.

'Go away, Sandra,' Alec said, quite gently.

The poor girl blinked again, blushed crimson and fled, leaving behind her a silence that was only broken when Jessica went off into a paroxysm of giggles.

'Your halo's just slipped,' she choked gleefully. 'Sandra will never see you in the same immaculate light again!'

'I never was a monk, you know!' he retaliated, then cursed his stupid tongue when all the laughter left her. He sighed heavily. 'I didn't mean that the way it sounded.' His half-apology was tinged with derision. 'You're the only woman who's ever been in the position to be caught alone with me in this apartment, Jess.'

'Another exception to your rules?' she prodded quietly.

He stared narrowly at her for a moment, then levered himself up, pulling her with him to their feet. 'I'll go and find out what's brought her in so early,' he muttered, and left.

By the time he came in search of her—respectably shirted—Jessica was dressed in her white gown and standing by the window in his sitting-room, watching Samson in the garden below bound about with doggy playfulness.

'She wanted to do some private shots before the day began proper,' Alec explained from the doorway. 'She came to the kitchen to ask me if it would be all right.'

Jessica nodded, saying nothing.

'I'll take you home now, shall I?' he invited coolly. The magic had gone. 'Jess——'

'Yes, please.' She spun around to find him hovering by the door, watching her with hooded eyes. 'I'll need to get in touch with Teddy,' she said, over-brightly, moving gracefully towards him. 'Inform him that I'm home and to get things moving on that audition...'

He was blocking the door; Jessica couldn't look at him. She had no experience of this kind of farewell. Her cheeks warmed, and she felt very foolish.

'I thought we might pack together,' she heard him murmur—a rusty, rumbling sound that came from deep within that cavernous chest. 'But if you would rather——'

'Pack?' Her head came up, eyes reflecting the sudden leap of her heart.

'Pack,' he repeated softly, smiling. He reached out for her, running his fingers in a tentative caress along her arms before coming to rest on her shoulders. 'You know,' he teased, 'pack, as in suitcases, trunks. Pack, as in moving out, coming here, to live with me. Will you, Jess, come live with me?'

She swallowed on a lump gathering in her throat. He was talking permanency, commitment of a different kind—a public kind.

'How—how——'

'How long?' he put in for her. 'I can't answer that,' he said quite honestly. 'I can't make predictions on where

we're going, because I have no idea. All I do know is
that I want you with me, living with me. I want to wake
up each morning as I did today, with you beside me. I
don't want to climb out of a warm and loving bed to
get dressed and go home in the cold and soulless hours
of dawn. I *don't* want to have to rely on set times and
preplanned dates when I may see you again. I want you
here, in the morning, eating breakfast with me. I want
you around—all the time, any time you can spare.' He
shrugged diffidently. 'What do you say—hmm?'

'Yes,' she whispered. That was all. Just 'yes'.

He scooped her into a bearhug of an embrace, and
the magic was back. Jess was laughing. For Alec, the
sun came out.

He prowled around her flat like a prospective buyer.
Jessica watched him indulgently, his baggy sweatshirt and
faded jeans more in keeping with his artistic image than
her golden Colossus.

He had only just returned, after dropping her off
earlier and going back to his studio to work for a couple
of hours. Jessica had showered and changed into tan
cords and a thick hand-knitted jumper in dark green.
She looked casual but expensive, her hair tied loosely at
her nape.

'What did Teddy have to say about your decision?'
The studied nonchalance with which he put the enquiry
was a give-away in itself, and made Jessica smile. He
was pretending a deep interest in her record collection,
back facing her as he squatted on the floor near her hi-
fi system.

'He was—resigned.'

Alec glanced at her over his shoulder, then away again.
'Hmm,' he murmured, his attention apparently en-
grossed in record sleeves.

'And what was that supposed to mean?' Jessica demanded to know.

'Just what it said.' He shrugged. 'Hmm. Can we take
some of these back with us?' he asked lightly. 'I would

never have put you down as a Motown fan, Jess. You've got some great albums here.'

'Alec,' she warned quietly, 'what did the "hmm" mean?'

He didn't answer for a moment, fingers flicking absently through the long row of albums. 'It meant—it meant—dammit!' he growled, coming to his feet and turned to glare at her. 'It meant I don't trust that twenty-per-cent devil not to try changing your mind! I mean—where's the sense in you turning down a starring role in a John Crowther film, when anyone with a little knowledge of the business knows that what you'll earn doing live theatre will be a pittance by comparison?'

Jessica eyed him gravely. 'Are you wealthy, Alec?'

That threw him, she thought wryly; he went all haughty on her, looking at her down the length of his arrogant nose. 'Comfortable,' he drawled discouragingly.

'Comfortable,' she repeated slowly. 'Well...' Her chin came up, and she showed him a strength of pride that by far outstripped his own. 'I'm more than that,' she announced bluntly. 'I work because I want to work, and not because I have to, which makes all the difference. You see,' she went on coolly, 'it means the bottom line reads: I can do what I want, when I want and how I want.'

'Now you sound like Teddy,' he said on an odd laugh.

Her gaze remained steady on him, refusing to be diverted. 'If I so desired, Alec, I could give up working altogether and not feel the difference in my pocket. Do you understand what I'm trying to tell you?'

He had closed himself away from her. She knew she was talking in a rather derogatory manner, but she had a suspicion Alec might be labouring under the illusion that she was some kind of lush; agreeing to live with him because he could afford to keep her in luxury. According to Teddy, his ex-wife had bled him dry, and in the kind of business they both moved in, money did tend to come higher on the lists of priorities than anything else.

'I'm trying to explain to you what Teddy already knows.'

She indicated towards an ebony-wood sideboard, where two large framed photographs stood. Alec followed her pointing finger, and with a questioning arch of an eyebrow went over to study them.

She touched her fingertips to one of the frames. 'My parents,' she informed him gruffly, then pointed to the tall, thin man with Jessica's fair hair and complexion. 'Chris Christhanson,' she said. 'The Austrian artist.'

'Jee-eez,' breathed Alec, impressed.

'My mother,' Jessica continued quietly, while Alec came to terms with the fact that Jessica was the daughter of *the* Chris Christhanson. The artist had risen to meteoric fame with his impressions of Nazi Germany; terrible, heart-rending paintings that shocked the world and now hung on the walls of great buildings whose owners never wanted that period in history to be forgotten. 'Anne Mawdsley, daughter of Sir Alan Mawdsley.'

Alec whistled softly between his teeth, recognising without her help, the name of one of England's most decorated wartime heroes.

'As a very young man, my father was caught in Germany when the Austrian borders closed. He eventually got back to Austria and, with the help of my grandfather, eventually here to England... But the experiences he witnessed before escaping lived in his nightmares for the rest of his life. His paintings were done in the vague hope that he could paint some of those horrors out of his mind. It wasn't entirely successful.' Jessica went quiet, looking down at the photograph for a long, sad moment, then went on briskly, 'Needless to say, when my grandfather introduced him to my mother, they fell in love and married. Helen likes to think that his love for Mother eased some of his inner torment, and I like to think she's right... They were killed in a skiing accident just over five years ago.'

Alec nodded, remembering the reports in the newspapers. 'Who is Helen?'

'My sister.' Jessica picked up the other photograph and held it out in front of her, smiling fondly. 'She's the elder by six years.' Her voice automatically softened into loving affection. 'She likes to call me "Mama's little mistake", but she means no malice.'

'She looks like you,' Alec gruffly observed. 'Who is the man she's marrying here?'

'Stavros Kirilakis.'

'Jee-eez!' said an awed Alec yet again.

'I spent the last three weeks with them, as a matter of fact,' she told him. 'Stavros is a native of Rhodes.' A strange smile touched her lips, and Alec caught it and wondered curiously at its source. 'He owns property there, and in Athens, of course. Most of his business is transacted from his head office in Athens. They spend most of their time there. But Stavros managed to or-ganise his time so we could spend my holiday together on Rhodes.'

'And you left them curious as to why you wanted to come back to England earlier than you should,' he drily surmised. 'What are the chances of the big Greek coming down the heavy brother-in-law on me?' he quipped, but wasn't really joking.

'Odds even, I'd reckon,' Jessica grinned. 'Big, power-ful man, Stavros. Deep-seated sense of family loyalty. He'll probably have you ceremonially castrated for daring to seduce me.' She smiled wistfully at the idea.

'He'd have to get past my Aunty Vi first,' Alec promptly came back, smiling because the tension had gone and they were back to teasing each other.

'That's a point,' Jessica conceded, her eyes gleaming on a vision of Stavros trying to get past a bossy Aunty Vi.

'I've just realised,' he drawled softly, taking the photograph from her to replace it on the sideboard, ap-pearing to ponder on a pleasurable idea. 'I could ac-tually give up taking photos for a living and live off *you*! Now, there's a tempting idea.'

'You would have to ask me if I would be prepared to keep you first,' Jessica pointed out. 'But, if the gigolo life is the one for you, Alec Stedman, then I think I should warn you that I can't stand idle layabouts, even big, blond, beautiful ones, so take care!'

'I could make you change your mind about that,' he challenged with meaningful intent.

Jess backed away from him. He had that look about him, like a lion about to pounce. He took a threatening step towards her and, on a high-pitched shriek, she turned and fled. He followed.

That he caught her in her bedroom, Jessica insisted later, was her bad luck and his good fortune.

CHAPTER SEVEN

THE move went without a hitch. Jessica simply closed up her flat and forgot about it. Moving in with Alec was more a natural blending of two entities than a way to solve the problem of whose bed they would retire to at night.

Alec worked in his studio, strolling in and out of the apartment between sessions to search her out with a command for coffee, trailing his protegés behind him like faithful shadows.

Aunty Vi welcomed her into the fold with a hug and a lecture about being good to 'her boy'!

'He deserves a bit of happiness at last,' she confided over a cup of tea. 'After the shocking way that woman treated him.'

Jessica became used to hearing Tracy Lopez referred to as 'that woman' by a thoroughly disapproving Aunty Vi. And over the ensuing weeks, when Jessica got into the habit of going down to the old lady's flat each morning to share a pot of tea with her, she learned a lot about 'that woman' and how badly she treated 'poor Alec'.

'He did everything he could for her; he was besotted with her—worshipped at her feet!' The old face puffed up with disapproval, and Jessica privately wondered at Aunty Vi's reading of Alec's relationship with his ex-wife. Besotted or not, she couldn't quite see him in the role of devoted slave, worshipping at anyone's feet. Not Alec, not her beautiful, big, golden Colossus. You worshipped at *his* feet—surely. 'And she repaid him by playing fancy-free with her favours, and making him the laughing-stock in front of all his friends!'

Not very nice friends, thought Jessica, if they could find it amusing to watch someone's marriage fall apart! 'Have you ever met her?'

'Several times,' pouted Aunty Vi, ample bosom heaving. 'She comes here . . . On the scrounge, if you ask me, though Alec isn't one for talking out of turn. But she looks the type—you know—the blood-sucking type. Beautiful?' Old eyes went skywards. 'I've never seen anything like her in my life! So dark and exotic—half-Mexican, I think.' She frowned, as if trying to rebuild Tracy's image. 'With all that long, black, wavy hair those Latin types have, thick and luxurious. Huge black eyes and a wide mouth—painted red——' The disapproval showed again. 'Tall, too, taller than you, dear,' she told Jessica. 'With all the right bits in the right places, if you know what I mean.'

'I've seen pictures of her,' Jessica murmured, deflecting the inevitable wave of jealousy. Alec couldn't have found two women more opposite in looks than herself and Tracy. Had he allowed himself to become attracted to Jessica because his feelings for his ex-wife ran so deep, and the scars she left him with still so raw that he had deliberately searched for the complete antithesis? It was a disturbing idea. It placed tiny niggles of doubt where before Jessica had felt only absolute certainty that Alec's feelings for her were as committed as her own.

'Well, then, you know,' huffed Aunty Vi. 'He's well rid of her if you ask me—ruined his faith in the human race, she did.' They both sat in brooding silence for a minute, then Aunty Vi added reflectively, 'She never stays long when she comes. Whatever takes place up there in his flat, she's usually leaving again within an hour or so, preening herself like the exotic cat she no doubt is.'

Money? wondered Jessica. Or to reassure herself that she still had some hold on his feelings? It was a sobering thought.

Alec told his version of his failed marriage with different words, but with the same bitter impressions running through it.

'We met when she was a raw beginner in the business, struggling to break through to the big time without knowing the first thing about how to go about it. I was young and arrogant, sure of my own genius.' He grinned at his own conceit. 'I saw the potential in her and offered to work on her—professionally speaking, that is,' he made derisively clear. They were in bed, lying comfortably entwined after making love. They did a lot of their talking here, in the pleasurable aftermath of passion.

'It took months of patience—she had a temper like a virago—firing off at nothing. It was one of the first things she had to learn to curb, that temper. No woman, no matter how beautiful, can make it in the glamour business without learning the art of patience.'

'You could do with taking some of your own good advice,' Jessica put in teasingly. She had heard Alec in his studio, exploding into fury at regular intervals.

'I'm allowed a certain artistic temperament, being a genius,' he vindicated himself. 'Whereas Tracy couldn't go around breaking up expensive equipment every time something happened that she didn't like. I taught her to walk properly, talk without making me cringe every time she opened her mouth. I bought her clothes, showed her how to wear them to gain maximum impact from her admittedly numerous assets. The relationship was completely innocent then, but...' His sigh held real regret. 'I suppose, quite naturally when two people are in each other's company as much as we were, it was inevitable that we became lovers. Then her career took off—and mine with it, I have to add. Everyone wanted her to work for them, and her blind trust in my judgement meant that I had the unenviable task of sifting out the sharks and vultures who hung around her, which caused problems of a different kind, because we were beginning to move in different directions and she was entirely dependent on me by then.'

'Not that different, surely?' Jessica disputed. 'Photographers and models go together in the natural order of things.'

'Oh, yes,' he insisted. 'It was the extravagance of the advertising and publicity scene for her. Whereas I had discovered this knack for portraying faces, and was wanted more by the private sector client. Different directions,' he repeated with a shrug. 'But we both needed a base to work from, and she still needed someone she could trust to take care of things for her. We were lovers, so,' another shrug, 'we married.'

'Did you love her?' Jessica quietly enquired, not wanting to know, yet desperate to. He had been talking so clinically, as though his emotions were never involved, yet they must have been to some degree, if they were lovers.

'Love?' He pondered on a grimace. 'Odd word, that. Covers a lot of things I've never wanted to analyse.'

Take that, Jess! she thought ruefully.

'Getting married deterred the ravaging hoards from trying to devour her,' he continued easily, unaware of the slight he had just dealt Jessica. 'Believe it or not, Tracy was quite shy then, nice, and we had some great times together.'

He went off into a world of his own for a moment, his hands idly stroking her naked skin while she lay, cocooned beside him, resentful for the time Tracy had already had from Alec, but certain of her own importance in his life now.

'The problems came later, when she didn't think she needed me any more. We still shared the same apartment, still made love if we happened to both be there at the same time—which wasn't often... Then, one fine, sunny day, three years into the marriage, she walked into the apartment and informed me quite coldly that she was pregnant.'

Jessica went very still, barely breathing. Alec—a father? Shock shot through her with a rawness that scraped across every nerve she possessed.

'She then went on to inform me of all the efficient arrangements she'd made to have an abortion,' he continued hoarsely. 'I was horrified. We had a row to end all rows. I said something crazy like, "You aren't killing my child, you murdering bitch!" and she came back with, "Who said it was yours?" Then, while I stood there trying to take in the fact that I'd actually been gullible enough to believe she'd been faithful to me—as I had to her—she laughed in my face and told me of at least three men who could be the father. I open the door, she walks through it. Bang! Door closes.' He made an angry, wafting gesture with a hand. 'I make to go after her, then think—what the hell! Let the cheating bitch do what she wants with her life from now on, I've had enough. She returns three days later, looking like death warmed up—minus pregnancy.'

He stopped again, and Jessica wrapped her arms around him, feeling his pain with him.

'I've never hated anyone as much as I hated her at that moment,' he admitted huskily. 'I chucked her out, and she went, taking with her—after one hell of a divorce—half my worldly goods, my pride, my self-respect and belief in any woman. Sick with myself as much as the rest of it, I decided to uproot and come to London. I'd already had offers, so it wasn't so impulsive as it sounds.'

'Have you seen much of her since?'

'She pops up like a bad coin now and then, in trouble of some kind or another—usually financial. She lives well, and earns less as the years go by. I sort out her problems and she goes away again.'

As Aunty Vi had said—like a cat with the cream, thought Jessica viciously.

'All the animosity's gone now. I mean, what's the use of it?' he questioned wearily. 'When, on the face of it, I have to admit to being more than half responsible for making her what she is. She still relies heavily on me in a lot of ways, and I help her out as best I can ... She— she gets to me,' he grimly admitted. 'A guilty conscience on my part, I think, for letting her down as I did.'

And I bet she knows it! Jessica thought bitterly. And plays on it up to the hilt!

'But the whole thing left me with a bitter taste I don't want to experience again. Marriage is for the birds,' he derided with a revealing deepening of his accent. 'The trouble with marriage is,' he went on bitterly, 'that, no matter how little your emotions are involved, that bit of paper makes you officially a couple, one half of a whole! It creates a bond you can never quite break free from. Divorce or no divorce, you still feel responsible for that other half. Call it a pre-conditioning of upbringing, social brain-washing—what you like! The fact is that the bond acts like a glue on your free will, keeping you stuck to that other half, no matter how many years you spend trying to break free.'

Or because the bond is forged by love, unacknowledged or not.

And it was that unhappy thought that kept Jessica awake well into the night, while Alec slept, unaware, beside her.

Then he did something that totally restored her faith in her own instincts. Whether her restlessness disturbed him, she didn't know, she knew he was asleep when he moved in blind search of her in the huge bed.

'Jess,' he murmured.

She turned to face him, willingly allowing him to gather her close to his golden warmth, her gaze sadly tender on his rock-solid face, relaxed in sleep.

'Jess,' he said again, and with her name on his lips he found her mouth with unerring faith in his instincts.

It was then, when he bestowed a kiss on her that came from somewhere beyond the physical, and searched for a spiritual reassurance that she, too, was in desperate need of, that all her fears died away.

He was not conscious of what he had done. Alec might put his true feelings in storage when awake and aware of what he was doing, but he could do nothing about the secrets he revealed to her while asleep.

'I love you,' she whispered when their mouths broke reluctantly apart, telling him then, because she too could play the secret game. 'I love you, Alec.'

'Jess,' he sighed, and at last she slept, serene in her unshakeable belief in what they had.

Teddy arrived in the middle of Jessica's third week with Alec, looking like the centrefold fashion-plate for the trendy male, wafting a slip of paper in one hand that contained the date for her audition—and a glossy magazine in the other hand which he plonked down on her lap.

'Well, sweetie,' he trilled, 'our dear Alec has certainly done you justice. There's something decidedly uncanny about the way he manages to capture the essence of someone—hope he never turns that charmed lens on me,' he went on consideringly. 'Dread to think what he'd come up with—dangerous devil to have about—don't think I like him—go and see Aunty Vi,' he decided with a bright smile. 'She doesn't look for hidden bits of a man's character—too busy doing more useful stuff like baking cakes and things.' And he was off in a cloud of male cologne, in search of something to feed his sweet tooth, leaving Jessica wondering dazedly what that was all about.

She picked up the magazine, and it was only as she read the famous name on the thick, glossy front that she remembered that the article about her was in this month's edition—and that it was directly due to it that she had met Alec at all. A soft smile touched her lips as she flicked through the covers, curious to see how Alec had photographed her. Then she sat, staring at the colour picture of herself in stunned disbelief, at last making sense of Teddy's ramblings.

'The Silver Madonna,' a deep voice said quietly from behind her.

Jessica stiffened instantly, unaware until he spoke that Alec had come in the room. 'Don't call me that!' she protested harshly.

'Sorry.' Taken aback by her tone, Alec stared blankly at her. 'It was a compliment. I meant no...'

'He called me that,' she said tightly, looking down at the photograph and hating it, hating it because Alec had unwittingly labelled it with a name she despised.

'Who?' Alec asked. 'Who called you...'

'Him,' she cut in bleakly. 'The one I told you about when we...'

'Ah—him,' murmured Alec, perceiving. 'Not in any complimentary way, hmm?'

Jessica threw the magazine aside and got up, walking tensely over to the window, rubbing her arms as if cold. Alec watched her thoughtfully, then reached over to pick up the magazine, studying his own work for a long moment, his expression grim. Then he walked over to her, drawing her gently back against him.

'Look at it,' he ordered firmly, pushing the magazine out in front of her.

Jessica looked. Her soft mouth twisted with self-derision.

The dark red dress she'd worn for the photograph looked neat, expensive and demure. Her hair fell loose about her shoulders, Alec's subtle use of lighting picking out the fairest strands so they shone like pure spun silk. Her eyes were a deep and piercing blue in the calm serenity of her face. And only that slight and secretive twist to her soft mouth gave a hint that anything went on behind the mask.

Yes, she looked Madonna-like, she reluctantly conceded, but there was something else, something far more compelling—something to do with that smile...

'I spent long nights wondering what was running through your mind at the moment I caught you like this,' Alec said quietly. 'It was in your eyes, in the strange smile on your lips. I felt, arrogantly, I know, that it was my right to know what secrets you were considering, because I'd caught you red-handed thinking them.'

'Yet you've never asked me.'

'I know,' he said ruefully. 'I think I was afraid of the answer.'

'I was thinking of you,' she told him softly.

'Me...?'

'Fatal attraction,' Jessica admitted wryly, shaking her head. 'One look and I was hooked.' In love, totally and irrevocably in love, she added silently. And it was that knowledge that was behind the secret smile.

'Me...' murmured Alec in husky acknowledgement. 'And yet you don't like the photograph,' he added grimly.

'She—she's beautiful.'

'*You're* beautiful!' he claimed, pulling her around to face him, the magazine falling unheeded to the floor. 'But you know that already. Jess,' he said less passionately, 'all I did was latch on to the essence of you—the bit you like to keep hidden from the world.'

'Teddy said that,' she told him, smiling tenderly into those topaz eyes. 'About your uncanny ability to capture the essence of someone.'

'He did?' Golden eyebrows rose in surprise. 'Then he's got more perception than I gave him credit for.'

'Thank you, old man,' Teddy drawled from the open doorway, striding in as if he owned the place. 'Would you believe a starving man's luck?' he went on to complain. 'Aunty Vi hasn't even got a biscuit baked! Bad timing that—should have known, coming here, been a bad-luck place from the start. Alec charms away my best actress lady so she won't go and earn lots of lovely money in America. Aunty Vi doesn't keep the cookie jar stocked for unexpected guests—and that stupid dog tries to bite me!' He sounded so offended that Jessica had to go over to hug him. 'Can't even get a consolation kiss from my favourite girl without someone glowering at me,' he added tritely, one eye fixed warily on Alec's disapproving bulk. 'Tell you, sweetie, bad place, bad vibes, upsets the old antennae, bad for the digestion, bad for...'

'Shut up, Teddy!' two voices chimed in unison.

Jess got the starring role in the play. She came back full of triumph, and went in search of Alec to tell him.

'What's the play about?' Alec wanted to know, his arm warm about her shoulders as he walked with her from his studio, sending his minions home with a carelessness that made them stare after him in amazement.

'Modern-day French aristocracy, where the outdated custom of arranged marriages still prevails,' she explained. 'I play the only daughter of a wealthy *comte*, who is about to be married off to an even wealthier landowner she can't stand the sight of. He's arrogant and condescendingly aloof, so certain of her compliance that it makes her seethe inside.' They entered the kitchen and Jessica went to start some coffee while Alec settled himself at the kitchen table, long legs stretched out beneath it, posture lazy on the too-small chair. 'The play exploits the pressures brought to bear on her by her family to comply with their wishes, and how she fights against them.'

'Does she end up marrying him?'

'Yes,' Jessica admitted ruefully. 'But for the right reasons, and only after she's brought the arrogant devil to his knees. It's a Liam Michael play.' Alec looked suitably impressed. 'Clever, witty, with a lot of soul to get to grips with.'

'And who'll play your arrogant devil?' Alec casually enquired.

'Antony Wade,' she announced, and watched curiously as Alec changed from lazy listener to a possessively jealous lover.

'Wade's a rake!' he snapped.

'So is Alec Stedman, so I hear tell,' she came back pertly.

'Bed scenes?' he demanded to know.

'In a Liam Michael play?' she mocked. 'You have to be joking! He's too good a writer to resort to those kind of sensation-seeking tactics to guarantee success.'

'I'll warn him off,' Alec decided. 'Wade's notorious for going all out to get his leading lady in bed. I'll warn him off before he starts.'

'You'll do no such thing!' protested Jessica, affronted. Then her temper subsided, as an impish desire to prod the sleeping tiger a little had her adding casually, 'If I can handle a great big ape like you, then Antony Wade will be a doddle by comparison.'

Alec straightened slowly, and Jessica watched with a thrill his head come around to face her, topaz eyes narrowed with intent. 'What did you just call me?'

She shivered deliciously. 'A great big—ape,' she repeated dutifully, then giggled nervously as he stood up. Her hands went up in front of her in appeal. 'No—Alec,' she giggled, backing away. 'I didn't mean it—honest, it was a joke—*a joke!*'

He caught her at the door, and Jessica shrieked as he picked her up and began carrying her through to the bedroom. 'I was going to take you out for a special celebratory dinner,' he informed her with insufferable calmness. 'But now I've changed my mind. We'll stay here.' He dumped her carelessly on the bed. 'And explore my "ape-like" qualities.'

'Yes, Alec,' she meekly agreed, running her tongue sensually over her lips as he began his arrogant striptease scene.

Golden brows lifted sardonically. 'Do I hear a note of womanly subservience in that tone?'

'Yes, Alec.' Her eyes were like two sapphires, glinting wickedly up at him. 'Big, golden apes are my weakness, I'm ashamed to say.'

'And what about big, dark, arrogant apes like Antony Wade?' he demanded to know as he came down beside her and began a methodical removal of her clothes. 'Are they another of your weaknesses?'

Jessica refused to answer, looking into his face with taunting stubbornness, mouth tightly shut.

'I'll make you tell me, Jess,' he warned silkily.

Of course you will, that's what I'm waiting for, she thought, and pursed her mouth a little tighter.

Alec was a despotic lover. He liked to control her every response with the finesse of a connoisseur, and while doing so showed Jessica new dimensions to their loving with each fresh encounter. He was sensitive, imaginative, and above all patient—sometimes brutal in his desire for her full compliance, but never cruel or selfish. He taught her to know herself so thoroughly that she bloomed like a rare flower in his hands. The care and affection he lavished on her lifted her spirits on to a whole new medium of delights.

They lived through the next few months in a state of mutual euphoria, and if verbal declarations of love were never made, then it didn't seem to matter, because the loving was there as an irrefutable statement each time they looked at each other. Everyone saw it and smiled knowingly. It became the great love story of the moment. The brilliant Alec Stedman and the beautiful Jessica Christhanson were an inseparable pair.

Their lives settled into a harmonious routine. Jessica went off to rehearsals each morning, and Alec went to his studio. They cooked together, bathed in Alec's huge sunken bath together, sipping glasses of wine and chatting about their respective days.

'Decadence,' Jessica had accused that first time he had suggested this way of relaxing after a hard day. 'Sheer decadence!'

'Naughty but nice?' he grinned cheekily, lying back in the foamy water, his foot running suggestively along her inner thigh where she lay supine at the other end of the bath. 'If you English could learn anything from us Americans, it's how to plan your bathrooms with a little more finesse!' He kissed his fingertips with mocking flamboyance. 'I can't fit my big toe in your poor excuse for a bath! It's like trying to soak in a washing-up basin for someone of my impressive physique!'

Having no argument to put to that piece of arrogance, Jessica resorted to diversion tactics by grasping the aforementioned big toe and yanking at it. Caught entirely off guard, because he had been lying there with his eyes blissfully closed, Alec had no time to brace himself on the slippery sides of the bath, and slid with a gurgling slosh of soapy water right beneath the surface.

What followed was yet another new experience for Jessica, conducted by a master in sensual play with all the delightful variations...

Days drifted by with the same easy contentment to keep them buoyed, and the only thing Jessica could see on the horizon that could spoil things a little was the time when her play opened. It would mean her working in the evenings, and she wasn't sure how Alec would take that. They hadn't discussed it yet, but they would have to soon.

But today was Alec's birthday, and she had no intention of spoiling things by discussing anything serious with him, today of all days. They were having a small birthday party for him, just Alec, Teddy, Aunty Vi and herself, and as Jessica got ready she felt the rise of childish excitement begin to run in her veins. Only birthday parties brought it on these days. It was the idea of a birthday cake and real sherry trifle that did it, that and the pleasure in watching someone open presents.

Teddy arrived early, before Alec had even come out of his studio. Jessica was just on her way down to see if Aunty Vi needed any help preparing their dinner.

'I'll get it!' she shouted out, to save the old lady the trouble of having to answer the door. She opened it to find Teddy standing there dressed in a brilliant white suit and black shirt and shoes. He had a gaily wrapped parcel in one hand and a huge bunch of out-of-season flowers in the other.

'Oh, for me?' gasped Jessica, taking the flowers from him and inhaling their scent with exaggerated relish. She knew the flowers were for Aunty Vi—cupboard love, because Teddy was her most devoted food-taster. But she couldn't resist teasing him a little.

Teddy blushed bright red, looked totally flummoxed for a moment, then tried valiantly to pull himself together. 'Er—yes, of course they're for you, sweetie!' he blustered, smiling like a Cheshire cat. 'I mean—who else would they be for?'

Mischief glittered in Jessica's eyes. 'No.' She shook her head, trying to be brave, and handing the flowers back to him. 'I can tell by your face, Teddy,' she said firmly. 'I jumped to the wrong conclusion and, being the sweet thing you are, you didn't like telling me so.' Already relief was showing on his face, and she couldn't resist the chance to really disconcert him. 'It's Alec's birthday. They must be for him.'

'But——' The poor thing was thrown all over again.

'Alec loves flowers,' she added blithely.

'He does?' Teddy glanced uncertainly from the gaily wrapped parcel to the flowers, then suspiciously at Jessica.

'Take my word for it,' she assured him. 'Give him the flowers and he'll be deeply moved.'

As if on cue, Alec appeared on the landing above, leaning his bulk over the banister to peer down at the two of them standing at the foot of the stairs.

Teddy looked up at him, shrugged his elegant shoulders in a way that said 'everyone to their own', and put the wrapped parcel down on the hall table before going up the stairs towards Alec.

'Happy birthday,' he said, holding out the flowers.

'F-for me?' Alec choked. If it wasn't enough that Alec topped Teddy by three inches and was easily twice his width, for Teddy to offer those flowers from two steps below Alec showed an impressive act of bravery, since Teddy was likely to receive them back on top of his elegant head.

Alec took the flowers, looked narrowly into Teddy's uncomfortable face, then even more narrowly down at an innocent-looking Jessica—and shrugged his broad shoulders.

'Flowers, hmmm?' he murmured. 'Thanks, Teddy, I'm—touched. Deeply touched... Ten minutes all right, Jess?' he called lightly down to her. 'Just get a quick shower before I join you—— Isn't this nice of Teddy, bringing me flowers?' Butter wouldn't melt in his mouth, he sounded so sweet. 'I'll—I'll go and put them in some water before they wilt.' And off he went, whistling happily to himself, looking ridiculous with that huge bunch of flowers hugged to his chest, leaving a deflated Jessica and a relieved Teddy watching his casual exit.

CHAPTER EIGHT

IN THE end, Alec was half an hour in coming down to join them, and by then they were already seated at the table waiting for him when he came in wearing a soft beige casual shirt and chocolate-brown, hip-hugging trousers.

He was holding in his hands the most beautiful flower decoration, arranged in a large, round copper bowl, which he promptly presented to Aunty Vi with a kiss and a thank you for going to all this trouble for his birthday.

'Oh—how lovely, Alec dear!' cooed Aunty Vi.

'I've been had,' said Teddy.

'*I've* been had,' Jess ruefully joined in.

Alec just grinned white-toothed and falsely at them while Aunty Vi, oblivious to the joke, spent time making room for the flowers at one end of the table.

It set the mood for the rest of the evening. High spirits were the order of the day, and, after they'd all eaten their fill and toasted Alec's birthday with champagne, Aunty Vi presented him with a tissue-wrapped package which, when opened, revealed a beautifully knitted Aran sweater that must have taken her months of painstaking work with her arthritic fingers.

Alec promptly put it on, and insisted on keeping it on even when his face began to look distinctly lobster-like in the centrally heated warmth of the room.

Teddy, gracious as ever, presented him with his real present, a deep, square-shaped box that had everyone leaning forwards in curiosity to watch the wrapping come off.

'I've never played it!' exclaimed Jessica the moment she saw what it was. 'Can we—after we've cleared away—can we play it now?'

'Is it like Monopoly, dear?' enquired Aunty Vi.

'No,' Alec said, smiling indulgently at Jessica's childish excitement. 'It's a game of general knowledge, sweetheart.'

'Oh.' The old lady was disappointed. 'I used to like playing Monopoly; I can't say I'm very good at general knowledge.'

'You'll enjoy this, Aunty Vi,' Alec assured her. 'Trivial Pursuit is fun as well as informative.'

It was Jessica's turn to give him her present, and she solemnly placed her offering in front of him and sat down, feeling unaccountably nervous about her choice now the moment had arrived.

As if sensing something very special was about to be revealed, everyone was quiet as the wrapping paper was removed. Even Alec was serious-faced, his movements slow, as if half afraid to look inside the tall, slender box. He kept glancing searchingly at Jessica's pale face, noting the way she was sitting with her hands clenched on her lap, the way she wouldn't meet his eyes. He removed the lid.

There was a long and breathless pause while he sat looking gravely down into the box, then slowly, with infinite care, he withdrew the gift and stood it on the table for everyone to see.

'Great Scott, Jess!' Teddy cried excitedly. 'Where the hell did you come by that?'

'It's one of a limited edition,' she answered nervously, feeling embarrassed, looking anxiously at Alec, who hadn't said a single word. She should have given it to him in private, she thought frantically, it was such a personal present. 'My—my brother-in-law bought it for me, at my request, from a sculptor on Rhodes.'

Unable to stop herself, Jessica reached out a hand to brush her fingers in a light caress over the gilded statue from the top of his proud golden head and down the

length of his superb torso, to his feet placed an arrogant
stride apart on his plinth of polished rock.

'The Colossus of Rhodes!' she named the beautiful
statue, almost jumping when Alec reached out to catch
her fingers, squeezing them tightly before carrying them
to his lips. She couldn't look at him. Shyness seemed to
have completely enveloped her. 'One of the seven
wonders of the world,' she reminded them, cheeks en-
chantingly flushed. 'Spanning the harbour mouth with
his great legs. Erected by the people of Rhodes in com-
memoration of their successful survival of a twelve-
month siege. They dedicated him to Helios, their sun
god. It was believed that, for as long as the Colossus
stood, Rhodes would never come under threat again from
hostile forces. He survived seventy years before an
earthquake brought him down... He's quite magnificent, isn't he?' she finished shyly.

'He looks like you, dear, doesn't he?' said Aunty Vi
to Alec. And the whole room seemed to shift on its axis.

'Yes, he does,' Alec agreed in a voice like gravel. 'It's
the most beautiful gift anyone has ever given me. Thank
you, Jess. I'll treasure it.'

It's a gift of my love! she wanted to say, but knew
she mustn't. The message was there for them all to read
if they wanted to. It needed no words to accompany it.

'Christos Vangelis,' Teddy murmured, rubbing his chin
reflectively. 'Christos Vangelis must have sculpted it. He's
world-famous for doing things like this... It must have
cost a packet, Jess,' added the twenty-per-cent part of
him, and Jessica laughed, releasing some of her tension
a little.

Her hand was still trapped in Alec's, and she knew
he was willing her to look at him. Her cheeks were
flushed, eyes shy and restless. It took some courage, but
she managed at last to lift her gaze to his.

He looked very grave but, as she looked anxiously into
those strange eyes, they darkened into topaz, taking her
breath away with the silent message she saw written there.
Alec lifted her hand to his lips and kissed her palm.

'Thank you,' he said again, but those eyes said more than that; they held a promise for later on that thrilled her, and at last Jessica's smile was warm and carefree. He understood! Alec understood and was acknowledging such to her!

'Let's play Trivial Pursuit!' Alec declared briskly, deliberately removing the tension from the room. 'Jess can help Aunty Vi clear the table——'

'Chauvinist!' accused Jessica.

'While I,' he went on arrogantly, 'clear away the discarded wrappings and refill our glasses. Teddy can set out the game.'

'Quite the little organiser, aren't you?' Jessica mocked pertly.

'Not so much of the little,' Teddy drawled. 'And be nice to him, Jess,' he advised, eyeing the flower display with trepidation. 'I'm still not sure if that's meant for my brains.'

'What brains?' Alec promptly questioned.

'I didn't know you were an expert flower arranger, darling,' Jessica teased.

'Oh, I'm expert at a whole lot of things,' he leered suggestively, and proceeded to pull his new jumper off.

'Alec!' rebuked Aunty Vi, not too old to pick up on his meaning.

'What?' he enquired, emerging from the thick woollen jumper with his hair all ruffled and an expression of bemused innocence on his face. 'I was hot in there!'

'Hot in some other places, too!' mumbled an amused Teddy, while Jessica blushed rosily.

They made up two teams for the game: ladies against the men, with Alec and Teddy scathingly confident of wiping the floor with Jessica and Aunty Vi.

But they didn't allow for an old lady whose veritable mine of knowledge was directly proportional to the number of years she had lived and learned without really knowing she had. She even knew how many different flavours there were in a packet of Rowntree's Fruit Gums!

'That isn't fair!' protested Alec. The men were losing badly at this point. 'I mean, I've never even heard of Rowntree's Fruit Gums, whatever they are. Select another question, Teddy,' he told the other man. 'They're not getting their last piece of cake with that question.'

'Well, I've never seen a game of American football,' Jessica argued with a smug pout. 'But you thought it hilarious that we didn't know what city the "Bears" played from!'

The ladies won hands down and, by the time Teddy left for home and Aunty Vi had gone off to her bed, the mood had seasoned into lazy contentment.

One arm around her shoulders, the other clutching at the figure of the Colossus, Alec led Jessica up the stairs to their flat, arguing quietly about who actually won the Second World War, Winston Churchill or John Wayne.

But, once they were behind their bedroom door, Alec turned Jessica to him and kissed her with such incredible tenderness that her heart swelled.

'The Colossus, hmm?' he teased softly, hands in a loose clasp on her waist.

'My very own sun god,' she murmured, touching her fingers to the taut golden skin at his throat.

Alec shook on an unsteady sigh. 'You make a man feel special, Jess,' he muttered roughly. 'Come to bed. I feel immortal when I'm deep inside you!'

As a declaration, it was beautiful, and Jessica responded to it with all the love she had in her. But as a truthful statement it later proved to be as useless as her power over the real Alec Stedman—the man, not the god.

First dress rehearsal, and Jessica was exhausted. Everything that could possibly go wrong *had* gone wrong. Fluffed lines, props that wouldn't do what they were supposed to do, doors that wouldn't open, lights that wouldn't come on. Someone dropped a heavy silver teapot on Antony Wade's foot, and he limped off-stage in a temperamental fit of outrage.

Jessica brought her small BMW to a halt outside Alec's home and sat back with a long and weary sigh. She felt withered. Her stomach had set up a nervous fluttering she knew would stay with her until the dreaded first night was over. Her muscles were stiff and painful, hyped up to a degree of tension that made her wince on the simplest of movements. She gathered her things together and climbed tiredly out of the car, her mind locked on to one thing—Alec's huge bath tub and the relief she would feel on sinking up to her chin in hot, frothy water.

So her smile for Aunty Vi when she came in through the front door was frail, to say the least.

Samson came ambling over for his usual pat, licking her hand in welcome, tail wagging lazily. 'Hello, old fellow,' she murmured to the dog, then lifted strained eyes to Aunty Vi. 'Hello, love, is Alec still working? I'm absolutely whacked.' She sounded it too, her voice barely carrying the length of the hall where the old lady hovered, looking, Jessica realised belatedly, oddly agitated. 'Is everything OK?' She tried to force some life into herself, straightening from the dog to arch her aching spine.

'*She's* here!' Aunty Vi whispered with unusual malice. '*That woman!*' she added when Jessica continued to look blank.

Jessica felt herself go cold inside. Ah, she thought wearily. There was only one person Aunty Vi referred to in that way. Alec's wife—ex-wife. What could she be wanting from Alec this time? Jessica knew a deep reluctance to find out. She had a feeling she wasn't going to like the answer.

'Where are they?' She glanced up towards the flat. 'Upstairs?'

The old lady shook her head. 'In there.' She stabbed an accusing finger at the rarely used drawing-room. 'At least he had the decency to keep her away from *your* flat! They've been in there over an hour—walked right past me as if I was the hired staff, she did. All airs and graces, the snooty little madam!' Aunty Vi huffed out a snort of affront.

'OK, darling.' Jessica laid a comforting hand on the disturbed old lady's shoulder. 'I'll go and join them.'

Making a concerted effort to pull her weary senses together, Jess moved to the closed drawing-room door, pausing only long enough to glance down at her casual white ski pants and pale blue overshirt with a white leather belt slung low over the slenderness of her hips. No doubt she was about to be made to feel inferior by the lovely model, she acknowledged drily, then lifted her chin, calling on all that hard training her profession demanded of her, and, with a flick of her hair which sent it swinging in a thick, snowy sheath over her shoulders, she opened the door and quietly stepped inside.

The tense atmosphere hit her like a million tiny darts the moment she entered. They were standing close together in the middle of the room, talking in low, rough voices that halted abruptly the moment they realised she was there.

'Hi,' she greeted lightly, the actress in her in full control. She went over to Alec's side, reaching up to put a brief kiss on his cheek—as she always did on arrival home. He was as stiff as a board, face like carved white rock. He made no response to her kiss, not with a smile or even a glance. Stung a little by his remoteness in front of the other woman, she moved away, her cheeks faintly flushed as she turned a bright smile on the curiously watching Tracy Lopez.

'You must be Tracy,' she greeted pleasantly. 'I recognise your face. It's very nice to meet you at last.'

Jessica held out her hand and widened her smile. The other woman nodded her elegantly coiffeured head, but made no move to take the outstretched hand, and after a tense moment Jessica let it drop emptily to her side. 'I'm Jessica Christhanson,' she introduced herself with a lot less geniality and a hell of a lot more irony. 'It seems Alec has forgotten his manners.' In more ways than one, she added angrily to herself. He still hadn't even acknowledged her!

'I've—heard of you,' the dark woman said, her voice a low and superbly modulated drawl that slithered like a snake over Jessica's skin. Long, curling lashes flickered and lifted to reveal those incredible black eyes she was so famous for; they went briefly over Jessica, then turned in a slow, dismissive gesture to the marble statue who was Alec. 'I think I'd better go for now,' she murmured drily. 'Call me, darling, when you're—sorted out here.'

Alec stiffened with a jerk, the air around all three of them unbelievably tense: the woman waiting for Alec to say something, he seemingly incapable of uttering a single word, and Jessica looking on in angry puzzlement.

'Look——' Jessica cut in unevenly, feeling very much like the unwanted intruder here, and mortified that Alec could make her feel this way. 'I've obviously walked in on something—private. I'll—I'll leave you alone again, please forgive the intrusion.'

She turned stiffly and began walking back to the door, hardly able to breathe as, with blow upon blow, anger, resentment, distress and humiliation bombarded her. If it wasn't enough that she'd come back from a lousy day of her own, to come in to this kind of strained atmosphere and have 'that woman' look down her beautiful nose at her was enough to make her seethe inside. Her hand was reaching out for the door-handle when Alec, seemingly coming to life at last, stalled her.

'*No——!*' His voice sounded like frayed rope scraping on wood, and it scraped on Jessica's offended nerves in exactly that way. 'No, Jess,' he said in a quieter, thicker voice. 'Please wait—Tracy?' He turned his attention to his ex-wife as Jessica turned to look questioningly at him, his face hollow with tension. 'I'll call you, hmm?' He was appealing for the other woman's understanding! Jessica felt anger land its bitter blow on her. 'Please,' he said roughly again when Tracy Lopez hesitated.

Those black eyes were going assessingly from Alec to Jessica then back again, and she shrugged, slender shoulders moving carelessly up and down beneath their black raw silk jacket. She was really most stunningly beautiful, Jessica reluctantly acknowledged. Her Latin blood was more than evident in her sultry face and blood-red lips.

'OK,' she conceded smoothly. 'You know where I'm staying, darling. I'll wait to hear from you.'

She turned neatly on one thin high heel and walked with the sleek movements of the trained model towards Jessica, her face a triumphant mask of feline derision that made Jessica jump away from the door before the other woman reached her. Tracy Lopez smiled at the revealing action, then let herself quietly out of the room, leaving behind her the most oppressive atmosphere Jessica had ever encountered.

They stood like statues, listening to retreating footsteps move slowly down the hall. The front door opened, then closed, and Jessica let out a long breath, unaware that she had been holding it until it came out on a soft hiss.

'OK,' she said coolly. 'What was that about?'

Alec made no reply, and she looked over at him, still standing in the middle of the room, staring out at nothing, the greyness of his skin an indication that whatever had happened here before Jessica arrived had completely overthrown his usual composure.

She gets to me, Jessica recalled him telling her once, and knew a severe sense of ill omen to accompany the recollection. Tracy Lopez had certainly 'got to him' today.

Rubbing a shaky hand across her forehead, Jessica moved over to a chair and lowered herself carefully into it, a deep foreboding draining the strength from her limbs so that every movement had to be carefully controlled.

He moved then—at last—walking over to the drinks cabinet to pour himself a stiff whisky. His hand was trembling as he lifted it to his mouth. He threw the whisky to the back of his throat, swallowed thickly, then poured himself another and sent it the same way.

'What is the matter, Alec?' she asked quietly, preparing herself for the shock she knew without doubt was coming her way.

He didn't reply, spinning away to the window, his back rigid, his large frame blocking out the thin afternoon light.

'She arrived from New York this morning,' he said, so unexpectedly that he took her by surprise. He hadn't turned, his concentration seemingly fixed on the view beyond the window.

'To—to work?' She was at a complete loss as to how she could help him. Her voice sounding weak even to her own ears.

He shook his head, the light catching at the golden streaks in his tawny hair. 'To see me.'

'I s-see,' she whispered for want of something else to say.

'No, you don't,' he muttered, and his derision cut into her, making her flinch.

He seemed to gather himself then, wheeling around to face her and coming to take the seat opposite her, whisky glass clutched in his hand like a lifeline, face distressingly white.

'Listen, Jess...' he began huskily. 'I want to try to explain something to you without...' He floundered, closing his eyes on her wide, troubled gaze. 'There's no easy way of saying this without...' Again he faltered, and Jessica jerked her hands together, fingers pleating into a single tense fist. 'We talked once...about my marriage to Tracy.'

Jessica nodded mutely. After all, what could she say? She had no idea what had been going on in here before she arrived, except that whatever it was had turned Alec from the warm and indulgent lover she knew into a haggard stranger.

'You know, Jess, how impossible I've always found it to dissociate myself from my marriage to Tracy. How I felt—*feel* responsible for her?' He took a sip of his drink, and Jessica watched him blankly, locked in a strange state of terrible premonition. 'I told you about the abortion?'

She nodded jerkily, knowing now with a sickening certainty that Alec was about to shatter her life.

'She's nearly thirty years old now, and aware that her career is on the decline. A model is only as good as her looks, and Tracy's are—fading.' He said that quite unemotionally, the professional part of him making an experienced judgement. 'Last year she met a man, a wealthy Italian, and—fell for him like a ton of bricks. He asked her to marry him, and she was floating on Cloud Nine, seeing her future secure with a man she loved and who she thought loved her.'

Whether Tracy Lopez was actually capable of feeling for anyone that deeply was debatable as far as Jessica was concerned, but she forbore to say it out loud. But surely the news should have elevated Alec, not sent him into the depths of despair? Unless of course more feelings were involved than a mere overactive sense of responsibility?

'I'm glad she's found someone to love at last,' she said, carefully watching his reaction.

Alec shook his head. 'That isn't it,' he said grimly. At least he had himself in hand now; his voice was clearer and less shaky. And although he still couldn't hold her gaze for more than a split second, he was managing to glance at her occasionally. 'Everything was set, the invitations ready to go out, when she was taken to hospital with what was diagnosed as appendicitis.'

'Oh, I'm sorry, Alec,' Jessica murmured in true sympathy, visualising that beautiful body marred by an operation scar. 'That must have been traumatic for her.'

'It was worse than that,' he choked, the anguish back. 'An exploratory examination discovered...discovered...' He couldn't go on. Instinctively Jessica reached out to touch him, but Alec flinched away before she made contact, getting up and moving stiffly away from her. Her hand fluttered back on to her lap. He was back by the window, staring outside again. 'They discovered an abnormality in her...the abortion...' he swallowed. 'The abortion has ruined any chance of her having children.'

'The poor thing,' breathed Jessica. 'That must have been a terrible shock to her.'

'He threw her over!' Alec went on hoarsely. And turned back to the room to stare at Jessica in glazed shock. 'That lousy bastard threw her out—refused to marry her if she couldn't give him kids! It floored her, left her reeling for months. She worked, she slept, she worked some more, then eventually had a breakdown.' He went quiet again, grimly contemplating the honey liquid in his glass. 'I never knew,' he said thickly. 'She never said a thing to me! We—we always kept in touch, yet she never told me! We were very close, dammit!'

His anger brought a surge of impatience to Jessica. This was all very sad, very tragic, but she was now clearly aware that Alec hadn't reached the bitter point of all this.

She came to her feet to face him stoutly. 'Where is all this leading, Alec?' she demanded to know. 'I can understand your distress. God knows, no one likes to hear of another's misfortune, no matter...but I'm sure you're not telling me all this for the sake of it. There's more to it than that, isn't there?'

'She's shot—had it!' he grated, moving violently to bang down his glass, then turning to glare at Jessica. 'Career gone, looks going, no future, events from the past ruining her chance at happiness. She needs me!' he stated harshly. 'And I—I can't turn away from her. I can't do it!'

So, thought Jessica with a strange absence of all feeling, it has come to this.

Her mouth twisted bitterly. 'Which means what, exactly?' she drawled sardonically. 'Have you invited her to make her home here with you—is that it? You've invited Tracy to come here and you want me to welcome her with open arms, is that it?'

'I'm going to marry her again, Jess.'

'What?' She stared at him in absolute bewilderment, the utter silence slamming into her disbelieving ears.

Alec looked sombrely at her. 'I'm going to marry Tracy again,' he repeated, very gently.

Jessica felt herself go cold. She shook her head in an outright refusal to believe him, and Alec looked back with pained eyes, refusing to take back the words that had just driven all the life from her body.

'No,' she breathed on a shaky whisper. 'You don't really mean that.'

His hand came out in abject appeal. 'I'm sorry,' he said hoarsely.

'You're overwrought,' she excused brokenly, shaking her head, refusing to accept what he was saying. Forcing herself to think, cope—understand! 'You don't mean it, Alec. You wouldn't do that to me—to us!'

No answer. Nothing but that haggard expression that refused to take back the words.

'She's spun you a line, a fantastic tale!' Jessica went on shakily. 'And—and you're feeling shocked, appalled—rightly so!' she allowed shrilly. 'But I can't believe you're that naïve, that much of a soft touch that you would go so far as to...'

'Please try to understand, Jess...'

'She's a lying, cheating, scheming bitch—and you know it!' Jessica cut in harshly.

Surprisingly, he didn't rise to defend the other woman. 'She's all of those things,' he agreed roughly. 'But I helped make her that way. I made her what she is, Jess. And I now have to bear the results of that.'

He couldn't do this to her! He couldn't possibly be subjecting her to this! Her hand went to her head, covering her pained eyes, willing the dizziness of shock to go away, leave her be while she thought hard, came to terms with what he was doing! She spun away from him, unable to stand looking into his pale, traitorous face any longer.

Then she was spinning back, hair flying out in a cloud of pale silk.

'But you love me!' she cried, tears filling her eyes, her mouth trembling because she was beginning to accept that he was serious, deadly so.

Alec stiffened, his anxious face closing up on her. 'I've never used that word...'

'You love *me*!' she stated thickly, glaring at him, daring him to deny it again, hands balled into fists at her sides.

Alec went white. 'But I'm going to marry *her*,' he repeated grimly, and, if it was any consolation, he didn't deny her claim a second time.

She stared at his hard face, took time in absorbing the agony of truth written there, and her mouth twisted into an ugly sneer, her lovely face suddenly taking on a hard, callous look.

'So now I know,' she bitterly mocked herself, 'I was nothing but a temporary mistress to you, was I?' Her voice rose along with her pain, eyes glittering with the onset of tears. 'You've always loved her! You never felt anything for me really! All she had to do was walk in here and...'

'Don't, Jess,' he choked hoarsely. 'You know that isn't true. I——'

'I can't believe you're doing this to us!' she cried, and the tears spilled over, one hand clutching at her bleeding heart. 'I can't believe you could inflict such pain on me!'

His whole body rocked with the agony in her cry. He stared starkly at the tears running down her cheeks, and let loose a strangled groan.

'Jess, she's barren—barren!' he grated. 'Don't you see, honey? If I had just stopped her that day—gone after her, made her keep the baby, she wouldn't have been ruined like this! I'd always run her life—every single aspect of it! I had no right to withdraw that kind of support at such a crucial time!'

'It wasn't your child!' Jess cried, appealing to him to show some sense, some sign of sanity! 'She'd been unfaithful to those vows you hold so dear! She had conceived someone else's child, then rid herself of it like any old dress she didn't want! You can't hold yourself up as her conscience just because she now regrets that!'

'It doesn't matter whose child it was!' he argued wearily. 'She had learned to lean heavily on me for everything. For four years—four years, Jess! And I can't rid myself of the knowledge that it is directly down to me that she is the wreck she is now!'

'And what about me?' Jess demanded painfully. 'What about me and what you're doing to me?'

'You're strong, Jess,' he said thickly. 'You'll survive. She won't, if I don't take her in hand again.'

Jessica looked at him through a haze of hot tears. Defeat stared right back at her, and she gave up, her shoulders slumping, then lifting again as pride overrode everything else.

'You're a fool, Alec,' she told him flatly. 'You love me,' she stated, head up, chin up, face a mask of cold pride. 'You love me and you're willing to throw it all away on a fit of overactive conscience that will have diminished by the morning, leaving you feeling as empty and ravaged as I'm feeling now. Well,' she took in a deep breath, furiously forcing the tears away so she could finish what she wanted to say, 'that is your prerogative. And I suppose I have no right to question your decision, since you've never once given me the right to do so. But know this, Alec,' she warned coldly. 'When the moment of truth hits you, and you realise just what you've done, don't come looking for solace from me, because you won't get it. I'll go and pack,' she finished, and walked with head high towards the door, willing her legs not to give away beneath her.

'Jess——'

She stiffened, but didn't pause in her exit. 'At least leave me with my dignity, Alec,' she whispered. 'You've just about mutilated everything else.' And with that, she walked out of the room.

CHAPTER NINE

JESSICA was packing when Alec appeared in the doorway, bracing himself with his hands on the frame, his face all ridges of pain and tension. He had the look of an emotionally shattered man. Jessica ignored him, moving between cupboards to open cases on the bed with a smooth precision that spoke of severe control.

She hadn't changed, hadn't even had that bath she had promised herself. The white leather belt, slung low on her hips, accentuated her delicate bones, the slender grace of her body as she moved. Hair the colour of pale mink acted as a curtain to hide the cold bloodlessness in her face.

Alec didn't speak, didn't move, but just stood there, filling the doorway with his rigid bulk, eyes narrowed and pale, glittering oddly as they followed her every movement as she went to and fro, carefully packing everything she had brought with her over two months ago. The air was laden with an atmosphere Jessica had experienced only once before, when her parents were killed. It was one she had hoped never to know again; it slowed the senses, numbed the nerve-ends so that a deep concentration was needed just to carry out the simplest of tasks. Inside she felt cold, her emotions under wraps because they couldn't bear any more exposure to pain.

Cases packed in that dull, dragging silence, she picked up her vanity case and carried it to the adjoining bathroom, where she continued the job of systematically packing away all the personal things she had collected there over the weeks.

Alec was behind her; he had moved from one doorway to the other, shoulder propping him up, silent, grey-faced, watching her like a man determined to witness the draining of their love right down to its bitter-tasting dregs.

Without once looking at him, Jessica finished her task, then carried the case back into the bedroom, carefully avoiding making any contact with his obstructing body, pausing only long enough for him to move enough for her to get past. He was big and lean and strong, a vital part of her own self; her nerves were already buzzing alarmingly, and she knew that to make physical contact with him would snap the fine threads of her control.

She clipped shut the cases with a finality that made them both flinch. Alec roused himself enough to step towards her, intending to lift the heavy cases from the bed for her, but fell back in white-faced dismay when Jessica turned on him like a virago.

'Don't touch them!' she grated out from between clenched teeth, eyes opaque with hatred and anger. 'Don't ever touch a thing that belongs to me! You've managed to taint everything—everything! Just keep your distance!' Her eyes slayed him where he stood. 'I'll manage on my own—just as I've always managed!'

Then, quite deliberately, her mouth set in a tight, bloodless line, she spun away from him and his blanched white face, and stepped across the room to where the statue of the Colossus stood pride of place on his dresser, and she snatched it up, looking sneeringly at it for a long, tense moment.

'God, Jess——' Alec's choked plea fell on deaf ears and, as she turned with the statue in her hand, he stiffened, eyes narrowing warily.

Does he think I'm going to smash him over the head with it? she wondered maliciously. I wouldn't give him such an easy way out of his home-made hell!

And, lifting the statue high, face nothing but an ice-cold mask, she turned and threw it deliberately through the window. There was the sound of glass shattering, and Jessica stood quite still, very calm, waiting to hear the missile land with a fatal clunk on the stone patio below.

'That's the trouble with tinpot gods,' she said quietly. 'They have no soul, they just stand there, shining, while inside they're dull, empty hulks, greedy to take, but incapable of giving back anything in return.'

She picked up two of her cases and turned one final bitter look on Alec. He was leaning against the wall near the bathroom, his arm bent along the wall, face pushed against it. He was trembling badly.

Turning, she walked out of the room, struggling down the stairs with the cases and taking them outside to where her car still stood where she had left it. She noticed Aunty Vi hovering uncertainly by her own flat door, but refused to acknowledge her, stashing the two cases in the car boot before returning into the house and back up the stairs to fetch the rest of her luggage.

Alec was still in the bedroom, standing over by the broken window, hands clenched at his sides, staring down at the place where the statue lay, snapped at its neck.

Jessica gathered together the rest of her things, turned and walked out without a single word. As she moved steadily down the hallway she heard the crunching sound of bone hitting wood, then a second tinkling of glass and knew Alec had just hit the window frame with his fist, loosening the particles of glass still clinging to the frame.

Aunty Vi had moved to the bottom of the stairs and was staring up at Jessica as she descended, her old face drawn with concern.

'What has happened, Jessica?' she asked unevenly, gnarled hands screwing up the hem of her pretty apron.

Jessica put down the cases when she reached the old lady, and gave her a tight smile. Old eyes filled with more tears, and Jessica had to swallow on the lump of distress she was trying so hard to contain, and she took Aunty Vi's ample frame into a brief hug. 'Don't get upset, darling,' she urged brokenly. 'This is what Alec wants, and that's all that really counts in the end.' She

sounded bitter even to herself, but she was in no fit state
to behave any better. She felt savaged, emotionally
stripped clean.

She went to move away, but the old lady clung to her.
'What happened? Why are you leaving—Alec can't want
you to go! He...'

'Don't——!' She cut Aunty Vi off with a harshness
that wasn't meant for the other woman, but for the man
who was the cause of all of this. It wounded her to know
that Alec could hurt so many people for the sake of his
own misplaced conscience.

Gently, placing cold lips on the old woman's cheek,
Jessica disentangled herself. 'May God forgive him,
Aunty Vi,' she whispered shakily. 'For I'm sure I never
shall.'

And then she was picking up her cases, ignoring Aunty
Vi's sobs—and the harsh intake of breath which told her
that Alec had overheard her parting shot from his station
on the landing above.

Jessica left the house, walking away without a single
look back. If she took anything with her to give some
brief satisfaction, it was the sound of the husky and
strained plea Alec had uttered as she left the bedroom
for the final time.

'Don't go, Jess,' he had said. 'Please don't go.'

She arrived at her flat to find Teddy already there,
propping up the wall beside her front door. He
straightened when he saw her, his handsome face grim.

'How...?'

'Aunty Vi called me,' he said gravely.

Jessica nodded; of course Aunty Vi would be worried
about her. It was nice to know the old lady had rung
Teddy—it hurt that Alec hadn't done it.

'You go inside,' Teddy urged her. 'I'll get your luggage
from the car.'

She handed over her car-keys without argument, for
she was way past the point where she could speak at all.
With a heavy sluggishness in her limbs, she unlocked her

flat door and went in. It had that bleak, unlived-in feel to it, and Jessica shivered, crossing her arms about her, moving from unwelcome room to unwelcome room, feeling cold, drained from the inside out. The stresses of her bad day had been thrust into the background by what had met her afterwards, but now they came back to add their pressure to her broken spirit, and she felt utterly wasted.

'I've put your things in your bedroom.'

Teddy's careful voice came from behind her, and Jessica spun around to smile a bleak thanks at him, realising for the first time that she was standing in the middle of her kitchen.

A cup of tea, she thought abstractedly. That's what I need, a nice hot cup of...

'Jess——'

'Jess—Jess—Jess!' She turned wearily on him, screwing up her eyes in agony and lifting a hand to her throbbing brow. 'God—I'm sick of the sound of that name!' Her body shook on a sob which seemed to come from the very depths of her, and Teddy took a concerned step towards her.

She threw out a hand to stop him. 'Please, Teddy,' she said weakly, 'it was good of you to come, and I'm very grateful that you cared enough, but w-would you go now? I need to be on my own.'

There was a short silence, then his voice hit her eardrums. Light, oh so light—his inane banter back on show. 'Sure, sweetie,' he trilled. 'No trouble, no trouble. Forget old Teddy even showed his face!' She'd hurt him. Jessica knew it and was pained by it even as his voice grated unbearably on her. 'I'll trot off—come back later when you're feeling more the thing. Can't have the lady upset—big night coming soon. Needs her rest, needs her——'

'Teddy!!'

'OK!—OK! Sorry, I'm going—look!' He was backing towards the door, and Jessica watched him in sorry agony. 'Look, going—going—gone!'

And true to his word, Teddy whipped out of her flat and was gone, leaving behind him silence, a cold, clean, antiseptic silence, and Jessica wilted visibly, dropping into a chair to bury her head in her arms on the kitchen table.

The play was a resounding hit. The critics raved, the audiences loved it, and Jessica found she could bury her aching self in the character she played.

She worked in the evenings, came home to a light supper, spent half the night tossing and turning to keep out the painful memories her tired mind wanted to replay, and the other half in a dead sleep of exhaustion which usually carried her through until lunch time and therefore left only the afternoons to fill.

He appeared third row from the front in the stalls, centre aisle seat, during the second week.

Jessica could not say exactly what it was that alerted her to his presence. Wounded instincts maybe, on red alert for any danger of another attack on her emotions, or plain old bad luck that she happened to glance outwards from that particular position on the stage where she could see the first few rows of seats beyond the footlights. But see him she did, and muffed her lines.

He was there again the next night, and the next, third row back, aisle seat, his commanding size too outstanding to ignore, his face with its golden glow lost in the shadows of the lowered theatre lights, grim, watching her, always watching her.

It took a week of this strange torture before she accepted that she couldn't cope. He turned up again that night, and her performance was poor enough to bring comment from the rest of the cast. The next day she sent him a note, hand-delivered to his studio, requesting, for her benefit, if he could refrain from coming to the theatre as his presence marred her performance.

He didn't come again. His seat remained empty, like the epitaph to a dead love.

She didn't know why he had come, and refused to consider his motives. He had sent flowers on her opening night. 'Good luck—Alec,' he had written on the card, that was all. The flowers were freesia and tiny star lilies, beautifully presented in a porcelain basket by hands that showed a sensitivity to their delicacy. Jessica knew instinctively that he had prepared them himself, how she knew she couldn't say, but she was absolutely certain it was Alec who had taken great pains over the lovely chinapot display. Other than that, there had been no contact at all. Teddy never spoke of him, even though she knew he visited Aunty Vi quite regularly, and she never enquired about any of them.

Two more weeks went by, and she began to feel more human, found she could look about her without that depressing lacklustre glaze clouding her vision. She began accepting invitations to supper after the show, from Teddy mainly. He was very kind, gentle, as if afraid she might shatter if he said the wrong thing. Maybe she would have done; Jessica had no real idea just how fragile she looked during those first terrible weeks. It was as if Alec stood like a huge golden shadow over everything, and her emotions had gone into a deep and personal mourning.

She hadn't cried. Had refused to give in to the need. Alec had wounded her, but not mortally. As he had said, she was strong, and would survive. It would just take time, that was all.

On Wednesday afternoon of the seventh week from the play's opening, Jessica was just considering switching on the TV to spend a lazy couple of hours watching one of the old films they'd started showing in the afternoons when the doorbell rang.

Opening the door, she then stood staring at her visitor in open-mouthed surprise.

'Would the kind lady happen to have a drink for the weary traveller?' enquired an affectionately mocking voice.

'Stavros!' she cried, and launched herself into a pair of welcoming arms, hugging him as though he were the prodigal returned, showering kisses all over his dark, handsome face, laughing, almost crying. 'Where did you spring from? Where's Helen? What have you done with Yannis? Oh, it's so good to see you!'

'Slowly—slowly, Jessica *mou*!' he complained gently. 'And be so good as to refrain from clutching at my lapel so. Italian suits come expensive these days.' And superbly cut, Jessica noted wryly.

Stavros Kirilakis was a man who wore his power and wealth like a mantle. His tall frame was made to hang quality clothes on, yet he could look just as vital in worn, cut-off denims and a plain T-shirt that had seen better days. Thick, black hair with the added distinction of silvered temples, velvet-brown eyes which could look so sleepy-sexy or pebble-hard depending on his mood, and a nature that was both arrogant and endearing in one package, all helped to make him what he was: a dynamic force to be around. This was the man who had chosen her soft and gentle sister to receive all the love and devotion he could give, while Stavros—well, Jessica had a feeling that Stavros still had difficulty accepting that Helen could love a life-hardened soul like him.

They entered her flat arm in arm, Jessica smiling stupidly up at him. 'Coffee?' she offered, containing her eagerness to hear first-hand about her sister and nephew until she had soothed the beast.

'Greek?'

'Of course,' she pouted.

'Then—yes, please. I am in dire need of sustenance after such a long flight.'

Stavros made himself at home on Jessica's settee while she prepared the coffee, sitting down beside him once she'd handed him his 'sustenance' and demanding information.

'I am here in London on business,' he informed her, sipping at the thick, black brew made just the way he liked it. 'A fleeting visit, I am afraid, two days at most.

Helen did not come with me because...' his pause brought Jessica's eyes up to his in questioning concern. And he smiled reassuringly. 'No—no, *pethi*, she is not ill—but—ah, how does a man say it without smiling like an idiot?' he mused fancifully. 'She is expecting our second child and I am, as you see, over the moon!'

'A baby!' Jessica shrieked, going to hug him all over again and only just stopping herself in time to save his precious suit from being covered in thick Greek coffee. 'Oh, Stavros, that's wonderful! A girl,' she decided adamantly. 'I insist on a little niece with golden hair and soft blue eyes who will wrap the arrogant Kirilakis men around her little finger for me.'

'My own feelings, exactly as I demanded of Helen,' Stavros laughed, his eyes softening at some beautiful and private memory. 'But she, practical as ever, says it is in the hands of the gods, to whom even I have to concede.' His shrug was purely Greek and philosophical. Then the indulgence left him, and he looked gravely at Jessica. 'Helen is more concerned about you, my dear,' he said quietly. 'And now I have seen you with my own eyes, I must agree with that concern. You have lost weight. Those are most definitely dark circles I can see around your pretty eyes, and the smile you wear is not a happy one, so, tell me the cause of this deterioration at once, so I may cure it.'

There is no cure for a broken heart, Jessica thought sadly. 'I'm fine, really, Stavros,' she assured him out loud. He would know all about Alec, of course. Helen had no secrets from her husband, and Jessica had written and told Helen the less painful bits of what happened. 'Helen mustn't be allowed to worry about me at this time.'

'My sentiments exactly,' he agreed gently.

'You must tell her I'm well—fighting fit!' She beamed him a smile that he didn't return, and Jessica subsided in miserable defeat. 'It—it wasn't to be, that's all.' The words were forced from her, by velvet eyes determined to get at the truth. 'He—Alec and I made a mistake. We found out we wanted different things.'

'Like what?' Stavros inserted gently.

She threw him a swift and sorry little smile. 'Oh——' she sighed, eyes clouding. 'Commitment, permanency, stability, love...'

'You—asked for those things and he—could not give them to you?' Her brother-in-law was treading very carefully. He, more than anyone, knew the depths and strengths of the Christhanson pride. Jessica, like Helen, could easily turn a fierce love into a fierce and unyielding hatred, if driven to it. He'd had personal experience of the vicious swing himself. He also knew the Christhanson temper. It rarely appeared but, when it did, it could wither a poor man where he stood—hence his careful tread.

'I asked for...' Jessica seemed to ponder for a moment, then began again. 'I thought he loved me,' she admitted bluntly at last. 'Though, to be fair to Alec, he never once used that word to me, or anything close to it.'

'By all means, my dear,' drawled a sardonic Stavros, 'let us be fair to your—Alec. Yet,' his gaze narrowed assessingly, 'I am sure I received the distinct impression from you that love blazed like the sun itself upon you both?'

'Don't be cryptic with me, Stavros,' Jessica said impatiently, sending him a warning glare. 'You and I both know the significance in the word "sun".'

'A certain statue,' he agreed. 'Forged from bronze and coated in pure gold which cost what you English quaintly call "an arm and a leg", privately commissioned from the most gifted artist on Rhodes.'

'A useless gesture on my part,' Jessica dismissed grimly.

'A declaration of love, Jessica,' Stavros stated gently. 'The fact that your Alec did not reciprocate in kind does not automatically rescind the message.'

'He threw me out.'

Stavros stiffened. That broken little statement had taken him totally aback.

'No warning,' she went on dully, almost as if she'd forgotten his presence beside her. 'One day everything was wonderful, perfect. The next day—poof! Gone ... I still can't believe he did it.'

'You—did something?' he enquired sharply. 'You hurt him, angered him in some way for him to treat you so callously?' Stavros was becoming angry, Jessica heard it in his voice, saw it in the way he got rid of his coffee-cup and turned abruptly to face her. 'Answer me, Jessica!' He commanded. 'What did you do to deserve such treatment?'

Whether it was his anger, or merely the fact that she had held out too long against her own sorely battered feelings—whatever it was—Jessica felt the control she had exerted on her emotions suddenly give way, and the too long suppressed tears filled her eyes.

'I only loved him.' Her soft mouth quivered. 'Th-that's all ... My big golden Colossus!' she added in bitter self-derision, turning her head away from probing black eyes. 'I had the gall to fall in love with your sun god, Stavros, and he made it loud and sunshine-clear what he thought of me!'

'Jessica——' Stavros murmured huskily. 'Don't whip yourself this way...'

'Hard luck, Jess,' she went on brokenly. 'Had a good time, but it's so long now. I'm off to marry someone else. I...'

It happened then, as Stavros pulled her trembling body into his arms. The tears spilled over and the flood-gates opened, pouring out the words along with the tears, until the whole sorry tale lay in a pool of grief around them.

Stavros listened with a steadily growing anger aimed directly at the cause of Jessica's grief, that ever-present Greek family loyalty rearing its head on her behalf to fill him with the desire for revenge.

'I'll kill him!' he bit out.

'You will not!' Jessica sniffed, knowing Stavros was quite capable of it.

'Not personally,' he agreed derisively. 'A man in my position needs to be discreet about these things.'

'Stavros——'

'I'll just have him—hurt a little, then,' he compromised.

'Ceremonial castration?' Jess murmured with unexpected amusement. 'He said that once.' She answered the question in her brother-in-law's eyes. 'When I told him about you, he said—he said he'd better watch his step with me or he could see his fate being a ceremonial castration. Funny, isn't it,' she went on absently, 'how well he read your reaction? He's like that—perceptive. He has an uncanny knack of reading people, seeing things others can't see—except where his ex-wife is concerned,' she added bitterly. 'With her, he can't see past her lying, liquid eyes!'

'A man's conscience can be a heavy burden sometimes, Jessica *mou*. Especially when his heart wants to carry him off in the opposite direction.'

'And conscience will win out every time, is that what you're telling me?'

'No.' He shook his dark head. 'That is not what I mean. Your—Alec may have been struggling very hard against his heart's desire—and hurt you deeply in the process, Jessica, but that doesn't mean conscience won in the end.'

An echo of a pained and husky plea uttered to her retreating back loomed up in her mind, stinging her into acknowledging a frail hint of truth in what Stavros was trying to say.

'He hasn't, after all, married his ex-wife again,' he pointed out gently.

Jessica stiffened away from him. 'How do you know that?' she demanded.

'Because, my dear, I made it my business to find out everything I could about your Alec Stedman.'

Typical, she thought mulishly. 'Typical!' she accused out loud. 'And who gave you the right to pry into my affairs?'

'My rights speak for themselves as your sole male relation!' He was instantly all haughty pride. 'My Helen is concerned about you! Your dear friend Edward is concerned about you. *I* am concerned about you! And your poor mental state proves that all this concern is more than justified!'

'I'll survive,' she muttered, getting up restlessly to prowl the room.

'Oh, yes, you will survive,' Stavros agreed grimly. 'Because your proud ancestry demands you will. But not by burying yourself in your work and avoiding the chance of beginning other good relationships!'

How could she even consider a relationship with anyone else when Alec filled her mind all the time? She hugged herself tightly, wishing now that Stavros was safely back on his beloved Rhodes.

'Your Alec . . .'

'Stop calling him that!' she protested impatiently. 'He isn't *my* Alec—as he made unmistakably clear!'

Stavros shrugged the rebuke aside. 'Alec Stedman still lives alone, Jessica,' he informed her carefully. 'With only a rather sweet old lady and a disreputable-looking dog for company!'

'Which goes to say—what, exactly?' she drawled, growing more sarcastic with each return volley.

'Which goes to say . . .' he took a deep breath, his beautiful mouth twisting wryly, 'that, no matter what his conscience tells him to do, he doesn't seem able to carry it out to its bitter end.'

'Perhaps she rejected him!' Jessica suggested bitterly. 'After all, meek, obedient, self-sacrificing wimps aren't all that appealing to a woman, you know!'

'Really?' Stavros remarked interestedly, trying hard not to laugh, and Jessica spun on him, blue eyes flashing.

'Yes!' she hissed. 'Really!'

This time he couldn't hold back, and barked out a laugh that made Jessica stiffen in affront. 'That is much more like the girl I know!' he commended heartily. 'Now I know the fighting spirit is not completely snuffed out, I can be at ease in your company when we have dinner tonight!' He rose to his feet, shorter than Alec only by a few small inches. 'I can't stand dining with a corpse, Jessica,' he drawled lazily. 'They tend to bore one so.'

'You arrogant so-and-so!' she accused ruefully, because he had made her smile when she had been ready to hit him.

'I know,' he agreed carelessly, coming over to drape an arm around her shoulders, then guiding them both to her front door. 'What else can I be when the most wonderful woman in the world loves me?'

'Getting round me through my sister won't work,' Jessica grumbled, but the kiss she gave his cheek was warm and loving. Then she stood back to frown fiercely at him. 'I wonder if Helen knows about your weakness for actresses when she's not here to see you?' she mused, tongue-in-cheek. 'Personally, I think it shocking!'

CHAPTER TEN

TEDDY called her up just before she was due to leave for the theatre. 'How does supper at Dino's after the show sound?' he invited without preamble.

'Not as good as a very expensive dinner at a very exclusive restaurant, with a very attractive man whose charm is only eclipsed by his dark and lusty sex appeal,' Jess answered teasingly.

'Who, where, how?' came the quick-fire demands, after a brief but telling pause.

'Who? A tall, dark stranger,' she told him mysteriously. 'Where? At the Fortescue, which even you have to admit is a better offer than Dino's. And how? Dial-a-Date!' she lied glibly, feeling light-hearted for the first time in weeks.

'What kind of answers are those?' complained Teddy, obviously put out.

'The only ones you're going to get,' she told him firmly. 'Now, I have to go or I'll be late...'

'Supper,' Teddy persisted by way of saying he didn't believe her. Jessica hadn't been anywhere to meet anyone worthy of all the things she'd just attributed her date with.

'Sorry,' she refused. 'Tonight, my handsome friend, I—am—taken.' And with that undeniably satisfying reply, she replaced the receiver, her mischievous smile back again at last.

Stavros came to her dressing-room after watching the play. His expression was ruefully impressed.

'I see you have learned the value of impassioned speech since I last saw you perform live, Jessica *mou*.' He lowered himself into a chair, quite ready to be patient while Jessica went through her nightly routine before she could leave the theatre.

She paused in creaming off her stage make-up to send him a probing glance through her mirror. 'Are you implying that my performance lacked certain vital elements before?'

'No,' he denied easily. 'Just that it has *gained* a whole repertoire of new ones.'

'Ah,' she drawled, understanding him perfectly. 'We thespians are rather like those absorbent sponges that live in such profusion off your native coast, Stavros. We have an ability to soak up all kinds of experiences life likes to throw at us—good or bad—and then reflect them back through our work.' She went back to the job in hand, fingertips moving deftly over her face, and Stavros watched lazily, stretched out in the chair as though quite at home in a lady's dressing-room. His black dinner-suit was elegant, his white shirt a superb contrast to his dark skin. His eyes were hooded by thick lashes, hiding what he was thinking while he in turn absorbed like his native sponge every word and gesture she made, assessing and translating them with that too-sharp mind of his.

She began on her hair, brushing it vigorously, then coiling the silken mass into a tight knot on the top of her head with a nimbleness of fingers that said how often she performed this task.

'Liam Michael is a clever man,' Stavros opined quietly. 'He has so accurately captured the senselessness in arranged marriages in these modern times.'

'Of course!' Jessica sighed, irritated that she hadn't thought of it before. 'Your own people still practise the archaic tradition, don't they?' Her smile was wry as she got up from the dressing-table. 'Yet you didn't allow yourself to be manipulated in that way. If I recall correctly,' she went on musingly, 'your family were outraged at Helen's appearance in your life!'

'Ah, but, you see—as Michael correctly makes clear in his play—you cannot educate your children to present-day standards of society behaviour, then expect them to

meekly revert to the ways of your ancestors because it
suits you!'

'Your parents had a nice wealthy Greek girl picked
out for you, didn't they?' Jessica disappeared behind
the dressing-screen, her curiosity tinged with rueful
mockery. She had met his parents several times. His
father must have been mad to expect the son of the father
to behave any less arrogantly than himself. It was in their
genes for the Kirilakis men to please themselves what
they did. Just as it was in the Christhanson genes to
survive at all cost, she added bitterly to herself.

His laughter came to her in rich bass tones. 'The
daughter of my father's fiercest rival,' he admitted ruefully. 'Black-haired, black-eyed—and black-hearted!' he
added with such bile that it made Jessica halt in pulling
on her dress. 'Spoiled, selfish, and utterly ruthless in her
determination to catch me in her poisoned net; it took
me a long time and some ruthless lessons of my own to
convince her—and our families—that I would not fall
in with their foolish plans.'

'Did they—hurt Helen?' Something in his tone made
her suspect his bitterness stemmed from that direction.
She had been only seventeen when he and Helen married,
busy with her own career and too self-involved to be
curious about her sister's love-life, but she vaguely remembered Helen coming back from a visit to Greece to
meet Stavros's family, looking decidedly the worse for
wear.

'They—tried,' Stavros grunted, and the grimness
threading through his tone made Jessica shiver. He would
not take interference into his life calmly. 'They would
not be so—impulsive a second time.'

Yes, thought Jessica. Stavros would have taught them
their lesson thoroughly. She walked around the screen
to tell him so—then was stalled by the admiring look on
her brother-in-law's face as he came smoothly to his feet.

'I am truly a fortunate man to have such a beautiful
sister-in-law!' he complimented her graciously.

'Thank you, kind sir!' She dipped him a pretty curtsy. Her dress was ice-blue silk, nothing more than a sheath of fine material falling from a clasp at one creamy shoulder to follow truthfully the slender curves of her body. Stavros picked up the wisp of silver gauze meant for a wrap and draped it lightly over her shoulders.

'I can see I'll be fighting them off tonight, instead of eating,' he mourned on a tragic sigh. 'And I'm starving for a good meal!'

The restaurant was crowded for this time of the night, but good taste and clever planning managed to keep a mood of space and privacy around the separate tables. Stavros saw her seated, smiling wryly at the looks of interest Jessica was receiving.

'The price of fame,' he whispered in her ear as he stood behind her.

'I don't begrudge it,' she answered. 'Part of an actor's success in this game is just having one's face recognised, and I'm not so well known that I get mobbed whenever I go out in public, like some I know.'

'That must be—aggravating,' Stavros agreed, glancing about him as he took his own seat. He would, in that single sweep of the room, have taken in every face and memorised it, seen who was worth remembering and who was not. It was all part of his strength, this sharp and ever-alert mind he possessed. Then he turned his full attention on his dining companion, and to all intents and purposes the rest of the room was forgotten as he set himself out to make her forget the emotional aches and pains that had become a permanent part of her life. He succeeded so well that by the time a delicious passion-fruit sorbet was placed in front of her she had managed not to think of Alec for a whole ten minutes.

As they talked quietly about their most favourite subject, Helen and Yannis, Jessica's eyes went wide with surprise when Stavros suddenly stiffened, halting mid-sentence, his eyes narrowing a little as they followed the progress of someone beyond her field of vision across the restaurant.

A strange expression flitted across his dark face, then he was leaning forwards and casually lifting her hand where it lay on the table between them.

'Jessica——' he began tentatively, eyes now firmly fixed on her face. 'If I am not mistaken—which I have to admit, I rarely am——' he squeezed her hand '—I do believe a rather large, rather determined man with the features of a certain god we are both familiar with has just entered the room and is searching for the sight of one special person.'

Jessica swallowed. 'Alec?' she whispered.

Stavros nodded gravely, and immediately Jessica felt Alec's gaze sharpen on her with a tingling awareness that ran right through her.

'Be calm, Jessica,' Stavros soothed quietly. 'Helios wears his golden shield up high in defence. You, therefore, must don yours also.'

Jessica looked down at the table, desperately trying to control her agitation. 'He won't come over, surely?' she murmured in something that came nearer a prayer than an opinion.

'I am sorry to tell you that you are wrong, my dear. He comes to impose on our privacy as I speak.'

'Damn!'

Stavros looked curiously at her. 'It is odd, is it not, that he should come in here, on the one night you dine here? Unless, of course, you have made this rather luxurious restaurant your regular eating place.'

'Don't be funny, Stavros,' she clipped. 'You know as well as I do that I rarely eat in places like this.'

'Then Helios is here by intention,' Stavros decided with what sounded like grim satisfaction to Jessica. 'Could it be that your Colossus has spies in your camp who will pass on information to him about your movements? And the fact that a rather attractive stranger is giving you dinner has reached his ears and so forced him out of hiding to come and inspect the competition?'

'That's just too fanciful for words, Stavros!' Jessica renounced in an angry whisper. 'You really do have the most...'

'Think about it, my dear,' Stavros cut in softly, still holding on to her hand. 'He certainly is not here to enjoy a late dinner.'

Jessica let out a shaky breath. 'Teddy,' she mumbled with sudden comprehension, and she was just about to embark on a full-blooded attack on poor Teddy's treachery when a shadow fell over their table and her senses went haywire when she recognised that bulk as Alec's.

'Hello, Jess,' he said gruffly.

Her hand jerked in the warm safety of her brother-in-law's, and she felt a betraying flush run along her skin. 'Alec,' she answered curtly.

For the life of her Jessica couldn't bring herself to look at him, and the tension began to build along with the silence. She sat staring at her wineglass while Alec stood stiffly beside her chair, and Stavros, unruffled as ever, watched impassively, shrewd, dark eyes flicking from one revealing face to the other.

'How—how are you?' It was Alec who broke the silence, making her jump.

So formal, she thought acidly. So civilised! Irritation brought her chin up, pride made her eyes look directly into his hooded ones. 'Fine,' she replied coolly, then spoiled it by greedily drinking in the sight of him, noting with a choked feeling the changes in him, the signs of a man who had been burning the candle at both ends. His eyes were darker than she remembered, and had a distinct lack of lustre about them, set deep into the sockets, his cheeks hollowed out in a way that made the beautiful structure of his bones look chiselled instead of carefully honed.

That he was as uncomfortable with the situation as Jessica was obvious and she had the vindictiveness to like it. He couldn't look directly at her; his gaze seemingly fixed on the way she clung to Stavros's hand.

'I need to speak to you,' he said stiffly. 'In private.'

His gaze shifted restlessly around the room; more than half their fellow diners were watching them with unveiled interest. Anyone who read the gossip columns of the tabloid press would know about their affair—and its inevitable breakdown. This confrontation was likely to cause a mild sensation!

'Just a few minutes, Jess,' he added roughly when she made no reply. 'That's all I want, just a few minutes alone with you.'

'No.' Her refusal had an unyielding quality about it, and his mouth tightened, that square chin with its deep cleft twitching jerkily. 'We have nothing to say to one another.'

'Five minutes, Jess!' he muttered harshly. 'Can't you even give me five min...'

'The lady said no, I believe,' drawled a super-indolent voice, bringing Alec's eyes flashing angrily at Stavros, who raised his eyebrows in insolent challenge.

Alec muttered something unintelligible beneath his breath, then made Jessica stiffen violently when he dropped down on his haunches, close to her side, careless of the curious onlookers, careless of everything as he brought his face a mere breath away from her own. 'For God's sake, Jess,' he muttered roughly. 'Won't you just let me explain to you about...'

'Send a letter,' she advised coldly. 'I've experienced your kind of explaining before, and I won't deliberately set myself up for a second dose of it.'

'I want to tell you about Tracy,' he persisted huskily. 'I——'

'Who,' another voice intruded, 'is Tracy?'

'His wife,' Jessica tightly informed her brother-in-law.

'Ex-wife!' Alec corrected impatiently. 'Jess——'

'My dear——' drawled a mock-appalled Stavros. 'It is decidedly *de trop* to be involved with a married man. It is not good for your public image, you know.'

'Who is this hick?' Alec snarled, slicing Stavros a look meant to annihilate. 'A protégé of Teddy's? He damned well sounds like it!'

Hick! Jessica glanced nervously at Stavros to see how he was taking the insult. He seemed, to her utter amazement, to be amused by it.

Alec's hand came down hard on her arm. 'Leave him, Jess,' he said urgently. 'Come with me so I can...'

'Take your hand off me,' she demanded on a furious whisper, glaring at him with the colour high in her cheeks and her eyes like glass. 'Have you still not learned any social manners?'

She was referring to another time, when Alec had held her too close on a certain dance-floor. His eyes darkened in instant recognition, and Jessica felt a quivering response of her own shake her fragile guard.

He removed his hand, but held her gaze completely trapped. 'Get rid of the big guy, Jess,' he urged softly, 'and we'll talk about it.'

She nearly gave in, nearly weakened to that husky plea in his voice, the dark pain mirrored in his eyes. Then Stavros broke the mood by making a threatening move towards Alec, and she had to put out a hand to stall him. Stavros instantly subsided, catching the trembling hand held out to him and carrying it to his lips. Alec's head whipped around with a snarl that was so animal that she jumped in fright. It all happened so quickly, spanning a few short seconds, that she hadn't really understood what was happening until she caught the wicked glint in Stavros's eyes and realised he was deliberately riling Alec.

'Get rid of him, Jess!' Alec grated, and the violence around them erupted with such force that Jessica felt her heartbeats accelerate in time with it.

'No—go away!' she exclaimed, glancing furtively around them. 'You're embarrassing me!'

'He's the one doing the embarrassing!' Alec shot back angrily. 'Where did you pick him up?' he went on in a snarl. 'If you're on the lookout for my replacement, Jess, then for God's sake find someone with more...'

'I would be careful how you put your opinion on my—shortcomings, Mr Stedman. I am not the kind of man who takes—criticism—calmly...' Stavros was not laughing any more. His quiet voice cut like a lash, and he appeared totally unmoved by the pulsing of aggression coming from the other man. 'Let me make one small point clear to you,' he went on silkily; the other side of Stavros Kirilakis had reared its cutting head, that hard, ruthless, dangerous side. 'Your—superior size does not intimidate me. I am quite happy to put a few cracks in that godlike face of yours if you tempt me into it.'

A short but loaded silence followed this whiplash of words, while Alec became aware for the first time just whom he was insulting, and he shook his head ruefully. 'Stavros Kirilakis,' he murmured drily. 'The man is the great Kirilakis himself.'

'And you are unwelcome at my table.' Stavros had lost all his humour and every bit of his amiable manner. 'Please leave, Mr—Stedman, before I have you thrown out.'

'Stavros——' Jessica appealed shakily. It was one thing her being brutal to Alec, but, oddly, quite another to sit back and allow Stavros to do so. 'Please let me...'

Dark eyebrow rose in cold mockery. 'This is the man who treated you like a tramp, is it not?'

Jessica winced at her brother-in-law's cruel method of bringing her back into line. Alec growled softly beneath his breath, and his teeth showed white and sharp.

'The lady is no tramp!' he bit out.

'I, of course, know that,' drawled an unperturbed Stavros. 'It seems to me that it is you who needed reminding, Mr Stedman, but, just in case you didn't get the full meaning of my remark to Jessica, then I will explain, quite precisely, before you leave.' He leant forwards, his dark face easily as hard and aggressive as Alec's, and to Jessica's overwrought senses it was as if the whole room swayed closer, so they too could hear

the point Stavros was about to make. 'I did not imply
that my sister-in-law was a tramp. I simply reminded her
that *you* treated her as one! She has been humiliated
enough at your hands, Mr Stedman, and she needs
nothing more from you—*nothing!* You are no longer
required, so—get out!'

Alec took it all without flinching, then turned slowly
to look back at Jessica, whose silver head was bowed,
her cheeks hot with embarrassment. 'You know I could
kill him, don't you, Jess?' he said quietly, roughly,
quickly, as though aware that his time was short and
determined to get in every passionate word. 'You know
I could knock him to kingdom come if I wanted to. He
can throw his power about as much as he likes, but I'm
not leaving here until you tell me to go. Jess . . . please
listen to me!'

'Go away, Alec,' she said tightly. 'Stavros is quite right.
You have nothing I want any more. Let's just leave it at
that.'

'I love you,' he said hoarsely.

'Too late,' she bit out, and her eyes seared him with
hatred. 'Go back to your damned holy conscience, Alec.
I don't want either of you any more!'

He went pale, searching her beautiful face with a
grimness that said she had at last got through to him.
He seemed to gather himself then, getting slowly to his
feet, and Jessica had to turn away from him, knowing
a pain that easily matched that which he was feeling.

His hand on her shoulder made her stiffen defens-
ively, but there was no sign of aggression, just a kind
of aching gentleness. 'OK, Jess,' he said quietly. 'Be
happy, sweetheart.'

'I never thought you could be ruthless, Jessica,'
Stavros murmured into the heavy silence Alec had left
behind him. 'Nor the type to hunger for revenge. You
left him with nothing, you realise that? Nothing.'

Nothing. Nil. Blank. It was what he had left her with,
after all. It had taken her two long and painful months
to see so clearly what 'nothing' meant. It meant a blank

page on which to begin writing afresh. If Alec now regretted his actions, then that was now his problem. If it took him the same two months to come to terms with that, then she could find it in her now to sympathise, but only for the wasted time.

She accepted a date with Antony Wade, and in doing so discovered that the sex-symbol image hid a shy and pleasingly amiable man.

'Play a TV cop hero,' he told her, 'and you automatically receive the hell raiser's reputation to go with it.' He had spent five years playing a gun-happy, bedhopping undercover policeman in a top-rated TV serial. 'It took me two whole years to convince people to accept me as a serious actor afterwards. I hardly worked during that period. My agent, terrified that my face might be forgotten, arranged for me to be seen about town with every presentable female actress who trod the boards with some success—hence my reputation.'

'And that proved harder to live down than the TV image,' Jess shrewdly assumed.

He looked rueful but unconcerned. 'I can live with all that so long as the good roles keep coming my way— like this one I'm playing now.'

Jessica studied his attractive face, and found herself doing so with new eyes. He had the look of a hard upbringing about him, yet, she noted with deep respect, he could convert all that hardness into a kind of upper class hauteur needed for the role he played opposite her.

'They wanted me to screen-test for one of the big American soaps last year,' Jessica confided shyly. 'But I wouldn't consider it. I had already had enough of working from a set on the films I've done—and all the false glamour that goes with it. It's all so impersonal! A scene loses its meaning somehow when you're asked to do it for the sixth time in as many minutes. It must be the same for television.'

'Worse,' Antony stated with verve. 'At least a full-length feature film has a beginning, a middle and an end, but...'

'Not always filmed in the right order,' Jessica pointed out drily.

'True,' he conceded. 'But a series of one-hour episodes seems never-ending—like being trapped on a treadmill. You begin to hate it, but the money and the notoriety act like drugs, terrifying you in case the next six episodes will be your last and your fix will stop. So you become obsessed with the current ratings, worrying yourself into an ulcer when you drop down a place— fancy being sent into a mad panic because Coronation Street or Crossroads stands higher than you on the charts!' He laughed, and Jessica laughed along with him, but the message held no humour and they both knew it.

Their friendship became firm. Jessica made it quite plain from the beginning that she wasn't open to anything deeper, and he accepted that.

'I know about Alec Stedman,' he said flatly. 'I know how it feels recovering from a disastrous affair.' He then told her briefly about the woman he had fallen in love with who didn't want him. 'She was older than me,' he admitted grimly, 'and not even particularly beautiful, but I fell like a brick and she treated me like a schoolboy with a crush... It was years ago, and now I'm heartily glad she laughed me out of her life, but at the time...' he left the rest unsaid. There was no need for explanation, Jessica understood. He put out a hand. 'So, friends, Jess,' he offered easily. 'Nothing more nor less.'

Her smile reached the deep blue of her eyes, and she placed her hand in his as if they were finalising a special deal.

Jessica at last began to believe she was getting over Alec. And if she found herself caught out now and then with a deep and desperate yearning to see him, touch him, witness the smile he had once kept exclusively for her, then those weak moments didn't happen as often as they had done, and she found herself looking outward again, thinking more clearly, discussing with Teddy what she would do when her one-year contract with the play was up. That big, golden man was slowly taking up a place inside her where all her most treasured myths resided, in that secret place in her romantic heart.

They were still playing to full houses every night, and she had a feeling the play was in for a long run, so there was every chance that she would be offered an extension on her contract; or she could move on to something different if she wished. She was again free to make decisions without considering others, and that made her feel comfortable, if not elated.

Then the unexpected happened, throwing her hard-worked-for peace of mind into turmoil once again.

CHAPTER ELEVEN

SUNDAY morning, and Jessica came crawling up from the depths of a deep sleep to the unwanted sound of the telephone ringing.

Dragging herself out of bed, she stumbled out of her bedroom, pulling on her dressing-gown, grumbling to herself because Sunday was her one and only full day off from the theatre, and last night she had stayed out until gone three in the morning, trying out a new nightclub just opened in the West End with Antony and a few more of the cast. So she wasn't in the nicest of frames of mind when she answered the phone.

It was a bad line, interference crackling into her sensitive ear. Then the voice came, deep and guttural, heavily accented.

'Jessica Christhanson?' the voice enquired.

'Yes, speaking,' she said with a puzzled frown.

'Ah—Jessica, this is Aristotle Kirilakis.' Helen's father-in-law. Surprise automatically straightened her spine, dragging herself fully awake. 'I am afraid you must prepare yourself for bad news, my dear. Your sister and my son have been involved in a car accident.'

Jessica felt herself go cold. 'Helen and Stavros?' she whispered, not taking it in, experiencing that odd numbing feeling one feels when hit with a shock. 'Are they hurt?'

'I'm afraid so, my dear,' the deep voice said gruffly. 'The car they were travelling in spun off the road trying to avoid a child. Stavros has concussion, and has not yet regained consciousness; otherwise he is, we pray, uninjured. But I am sorry to have to tell you that Helen's injuries are more serious.'

All the colour drained from Jessica's face, and she had to reach out with her free hand for support from the nearby wall. Helen—injured! she thought wildly. Helen—hurt!

'How—how bad is she?' she whispered, unable to give her voice any volume at all.

'We think she will lose the child she carries,' Aristotle informed her grimly, breaking up a little over the words. 'She has some broken bones, but it is the problem of internal injury which concerns the doctors the most . . . I am sorry, dear, to be the bearer of such—upsetting news.'

'When did it happen?' Trying desperately to grapple with the shock, Jessica forced herself to concentrate.

'We are at midday here in Athens. The accident occurred at nine o'clock this morning. I apologise for the delay in contacting you, Jessica, but I wanted to be certain of my facts before I called you.'

Athens was two hours ahead of London. While she had been sleeping peacefully in her bed, Helen and Stavros had been lying hurt!

'It happened in Athens?' Jessica was immediately planning how she would get to the Greek capital by the quickest route when Aristotle cut in with a guttural negative.

'I confuse you,' he apologised with a self-condemning sigh. 'Please forgive an old man's troubled mind. I am speaking to you from Athens. My son and his family were at their villa on Rhodes. Stavros and Helen were on their way to church this morning—you must remember, dear, how treacherous the road to Lindos can be after one of our violent summer storms? A child ran out in front of the car; Stavros took evasive action and the car spun on the wet surface. They—they left the road just south of Kalathos. The car turned over, trapping Stavros inside for a while, but unfortunately Helen was thrown out, and——'

He couldn't go on, and a distressed silence held them both for a terrible moment while the scene Aristotle

Kirilakis had just described flickered horribly through both their minds.

'Yannis?' Jessica asked fearfully. Aristotle hadn't mentioned his grandson at all.

'He was not with them, Jessica,' the deep voice said with gruff relief. 'He had stayed behind at the villa with his nurse. If we must be thankful for anything, then I suppose it is for that alone. The boy is still at home, but he is fretting, and my wife and I are about to fly out the moment I have completed this call...I...' He paused, and Jessica waited with a heavy heart for what else was to come. 'I cannot, my dear, stress to you enough how imperative it is that you come as soon as you can.'

'H-Helen?' she whispered.

'*Neh*—yes, I am afraid so,' he said hoarsely, and Jessica closed her eyes as the walls threatened to close in on her.

'I'll—I'll come straight away,' she said thickly. 'Just as soon as I can...'

'I have made some arrangements.' The Greek cut in briskly, deliberately making an effort to sound more productive. 'A plane has been put at your disposal.' He named a private airport just outside London, and Jessica wrote it down with a shaking hand, having a vague memory of it being the airport Stavros and Helen used when they flew in to England. 'It will be ready to take off at two o'clock, your time. If you cannot arrange to be there by that time, then you must call up the airport and inform them of this so the pilot can make the necessary alterations in his flight plan. You have that, Jessica?'

'Yes—yes,' she said huskily, trying her best to follow his lead and appear more in control of herself than she actually was.

'Good. There will be a car waiting for you when you land in Rhodes, to take you directly to the hospital. Anything—anything at all you need, dear, you must not hesitate to call me.' He gave her several phone numbers where she could contact him, and Jessica wrote them down quickly. 'Your sister has a very special place in my affections, Jessica,' he then murmured gruffly. 'My son was truly a fortunate man when he found her; I—we pray, dear, we pray very hard for her safe journey through this perilous time.'

And that, thought Jessica heavily as she replaced the receiver, said all the things Mr Kirilakis hadn't been able to put into words. Helen was gravely ill.

Feeling numbed with shock, she stumbled over to a chair and lowered herself into it, struggling with the need to be calm and clear-headed if she were to do all the things which would need doing before she could think of catching that important two o'clock flight. There were people to call, apologies to make, packing to do.

Teddy. His fashion-plate image appeared like the answer to her prayers in front of her. And she got up, refusing to acknowledge the tremblings of her limbs, to call her agent. He answered almost immediately.

'Hi, sweetie!' he trilled happily. 'To what do I owe this honour? My favourite girl usually likes to hibernate on a Sunday!'

'I've just received some bad news,' she told him quietly, then quickly went on to outline the details for him. 'I'm going to need an urgent leave of absence from the play,' she went on shakily. 'Liam Michael will need warning. He'll want to put my stand-in through her paces before Monday when the play opens again.'

'Easy does it, Jess.' Teddy's asinine manner vanished, and the sharper, more capable Teddy came to her aid. 'Leave all that to me. You just get yourself packed and ready to leave by—one o'clock? I'll drive you to the airport, so all you have to do is think of the essentials and leave the trivialities to me.'

'You're a dear, Teddy,' she said thickly. 'I don't know what I would do without you.'

'Survive,' he said wryly, unaware of the painful chord he struck in her with that remark. 'You're no feeble creature, Jess. And remember at the same time that your sister has that same quality. She'll survive too, Jess. You wait and see.'

A sudden tremor shook her, more a wave of weak yearning that held her throat locked on a block of tears and she whispered hoarsely into the phone's mouthpiece. 'Teddy... Alec, can you——' She stopped herself in time, shocking herself by the trick her cruel emotions had just played on her. 'It doesn't matter,' she added quickly, dragging herself back together again. 'I'll see you at one o'clock, and thank you, darling.'

'No trouble, Jess,' Teddy murmured. 'Don't worry more than you have to, and... I'll be with you as soon as I can make it.'

Why had she said that? she wondered dazedly as she replaced the receiver with a hand that shook badly. What, with all the worries and fears rushing through her just now, had made her yearn for Alec so much that she could actually voice as much to Teddy?

Jess shook her head wearily, so utterly confused with herself that it seemed useless trying to analyse the workings of an obviously demented mind!

The hour from twelve o'clock onwards dragged intolerably. She had packed a single suitcase, and placed it ready by the flat door, showered and dressed in a lightweight chambray suit with a full skirt gathered on to a hip-hugging yoke, the jacket tailored to fit into her slim waist made of the same pale blue material. She had braided her hair in a loose plait and applied a thin coat of make-up in the hope that it would disguise some of the strain she knew she was showing on her face. And now she sat, waiting for Teddy with an outward appearance of complete calm, while her insides cloyed with a desperate desire to be off, doing something—anything so long as she didn't have time to sit still and think, worry, grapple with the thousand and one fears this kind of situation taunted the imagination with.

So it was with a great sigh of relief that she jumped to her feet when her doorbell rang fifteen minutes earlier than expected, and she rushed to the door, flinging it open with a desire to throw herself gratefully on Teddy.

But her intentions died a swift and confusing death when, instead of finding Teddy standing indolently on her threshold, she found a large, infinitely familiar frame standing there, serious-faced, and hooded-eyed, looking as big and golden and solid as she always imagined him.

'Hello, Jess,' Alec greeted huskily.

'Alec...' A trembling hand lifted to her mouth, covering up the strangled sound she made just before the tears came to sting her wide, staring eyes. Then she was throwing herself at him, with all the distress she had held in check since the phone call from Greece, and Alec caught her with a muttered curse, holding her tightly, rocking her like a child, to and fro, as he felt the awful tremors rip through her slender frame.

'It's all right,' he soothed her with a tenderness that only increased her distress. 'It's all right, Jess. Everything's going to be fine, you'll see.'

The gruff, comforting words washed over her, and she clung shamelessly to him, allowing him to ease her into her flat and close the door behind him, letting his warm arms enfold her in a bearhug of an embrace while she sobbed the whole sorry story out into his shoulder.

'I'm so afraid!' she choked. 'Helen is all I've got. I can't lose her! I can't...'

'You've got me, Jess.' His mouth was warm on her temple, soothing, like a balm to her aching fears. 'I'll always be here for you, any time you need me.'

'No...' Jessica pulled away from the warm haven of his arms, his husky declaration bringing the heaviness of reality back with it. Alec let her go, his hands dropping to his sides in a weary gesture, understanding the meaning of the single negative and watching her grimly try to pull herself together again. 'Why—why are you here, Alec?'

He didn't answer for a moment, and Jessica made a play at wiping away her tears with her handkerchief so that she didn't weaken and look up at him. She knew by his uneven breathing that he wanted to talk about things she didn't want to hear. Not now, not when...

'Teddy called me,' he said after a moment, acknowledging her right to put her concern for her family above their own problems. 'He—he had the idea that you might be grateful for my support, so here I am.' There was enough derision in his tone to tell her how uncertain he had been of his welcome. 'I assured Teddy I would see you were taken good care of while he sorted out the more—impersonal problems needing attention—is this your case, Jess?' He bent to pick up the ready suitcase.

'Teddy sent you?' she asked in surprise, then remembered what she had almost said to him on the phone and felt her cheeks flush revealingly. Damn Teddy, she thought. He always was too quick-witted for her to fool. Alec was looking at her narrowly, wondering, no doubt, what was going through her mind to make her colour up like that. She turned her attention quickly to the suitcase dangling from his hand. 'Yes—er—yes, that's it.'

'Then shall we go?' He took her arm, turning her towards the door. 'Passport? Everything you need like that in your bag?'

Jessica nodded dully. 'I think so.'

'Then let's go. My car's outside. We'll have to move if we want to take off on time.'

That brought her up short as Alec was about to guide her out of the door, and she looked up at him, startled. 'Y-you're coming to Greece with me?' she asked, barely daring to hope it was so, and knowing guiltily that she would be too proud to ask him to accompany her, no matter how desperately she wanted him with her.

Yellow eyes darkened to topaz. 'You need me, Jess,' he said gruffly. 'You may not know you do, but you need someone with you during those long hours of flying.'

Her pale face crumpled again, on a momentary loss of control, and her hand, pure white and trembling, almost without her being aware of it, touched cold fingertips to his chest, feeling the steady pounding of his heart beneath his thin white shirt, his warmth, his presence so utterly reassuring to her. She smiled sadly, nodding her head in mute compliance.

'Thank you,' she whispered thickly. 'Thank you, Alec.'

'Don't thank me,' he muttered, swallowing tensely, as though her gratitude hurt him. 'You owe me nothing— nothing at all.'

He led her out to the car, seeing her safely inside and placing her case in the boot before coming around to climb in beside her. Without another word, face closed and set, he put the car into smooth motion.

Jessica closed her eyes, leaning back in the seat in a way that showed how exhausting worry could be to the senses. Alec drove in silence, taking them out of the street she lived in and melting into the mainstream of London traffic. They had been driving for about five minutes when she took him by surprise by placing her hand on his knee. 'Thank you anyway, Alec,' she said quietly. 'Having you with me means an awful lot to me.'

This time he made no answering remark. It was as if the seriousness of the situation rendered ineffectual everything that stood between them, and Alec accepted the truce, with all its tenuous links, without testing them with more words.

The journey was long and tedious, and even the relative luxury of a Kirilakis private jet couldn't make the six long hours it took to arrive on Rhodes pass by any quicker. But they landed to the priority treatment the Kirilakis name commanded, skirting all the usual formalities to find themselves being ushered into a waiting limousine before they'd had a chance to get their bearings.

It was dark outside. The ten o'clock Greek sky was a cloth of navy blue velvet speckled with glittering diamonds; the air was so warm that it caressed the skin like the soft touch of a lover. Jessica shivered delicately at the unbidden conjuring up of the image, the man beside her unknowingly guilty of stimulating such unwanted notions.

'Cold?' Alec enquired, noting the shiver.

Jessica shook her head with a strange smile.

He had been so kind and quietly reassuring throughout the whole journey, never once trying to jolt her out of her abstraction, speaking only when she spoke to him, keeping the topics firmly away from anything even vaguely personal to them. She had given him a less emotional description of the accident, and he had listened gravely, comforting without attempting to utter any of the inane platitudes times like these resurrect. And Jessica had in turn leaned heavily on his support, shamelessly almost, clinging to him like the lifeline he had once been to her.

His hand was lightly clasping hers now, big, strong and warm, and she squeezed it gently to reassure him that she was all right. Words had been kept to a minimum between them, and Jessica realised her reluctance to talk was because she was mentally armouring herself for what might meet her. Concern for Helen and Stavros filled her mind. The loss of composure back in London seemed a long time ago.

The car whisked smoothly through the people-packed resorts of Ixia and Trianda, then began climbing the curving line of road that clung to the side of the rock protrusion which hid Rhodes Town from view: the sea on one side, swishing lazily against the rocks below, and a rugged cliff-face on the other.

The car carried them smoothly over the top of the rise, and Jessica became aware of her companion's sudden stirring beside her, blinking fully alert when she caught his involuntary gasp as the ancient city of Rhodes came into view.

Rhodes Palace stood proudly on its own hill, dominating the skyline, its ancient stone walls lit up with glowing majesty.

'The Palace of the Grand Masters,' she informed him softly. 'Rhodes is a colourful mixture of a dozen different civilisations, some of them so old it seems impossible to comprehend, and they've all left their mark on the island.' They were slowing down at the huge intersection where the traffic converged from all directions of the town. Their driver filtered expertly through to take them off towards the newer section of the town where the hospital was situated, and the Palace was once against lost from view by the rows of modern hotels and roadside tavernas. 'The old town goes back to mediaeval times, but the new town—where all the commercial buildings stand—are barely a hundred years old.'

'It sounds a fascinating place,' Alec murmured, forgetting the sombre reasons for them being here to peer interestedly out of the window at the gaily lit tavernas, people laughing, singing, enjoying themselves in that marvellously simple Greek way.

'Brought your camera?' Jess enquired with a flash of her old humour.

Alec turned a lopsided smile on her. 'Would I move without it?' he threw back ruefully.

Jessica sighed wistfully, eyes glazing over again. 'I love this island,' she confided softly. 'I love its people and its legends and its air of magical mystery... I love the scent of citrus in the air, and the beautiful giant red rose Rhodes gets her name from. I *hate* coming back here with sadness in my heart!' she exclaimed on a muffled choke. 'No one should be hurt or unhappy here.'

Alec said nothing, but his hand tightened on hers, and Jessica knew a deep sense of comfort from his sturdy presence.

'We have arrived, Miss Christhanson,' the driver informed her. Jessica glanced out of the window, and the ugly tension returned.

Alec was out of the car first, helping her to alight, and holding on to her arm as they turned towards the lit hospital doors.

'I don't think I want to go in,' she whispered tremulously, the fear of knowing the truth suddenly too frightening to consider. Again Alec wisely remained silent, winding his arm around her shoulders and pulling her against his solid warmth, giving her what she needed the most: his strength and courage.

The first person she saw once inside the clean hospital reception was Aristotle Kirilakis, looking tired and drawn. He saw her almost immediately, and a strained smile of welcome touched his hard features as he began walking towards them, tall and as proud as his arrogant son, hair pure white, body a perfectly co-ordinated package of lean power.

'Jessica, my dear.' He reached her and took her into a brief embrace. 'You made good time ... good time.'

'Helen?' she enquired fearfully. He looked so dreadfully grim.

'She is—still with us,' he quickly assured her. 'But——' the white head shook slowly, brown eyes grave on Jessica's anxious blue ones '—the child—he is gone.' His voice was gentle.

Tears sprung to her eyes, her bloodless mouth quivering, and she felt Alec move closer to her, his presence meant to comfort—and too imposing to go unnoticed by the Greek; Aristotle looked at him in curiosity.

'Alec Stedman, sir,' he introduced himself, offering his hand. 'A—close friend of Miss Christhanson.' His manner was so respectful of the older man that Jessica felt her heart swell with pride for him.

Aristotle eyed them both wisely for a moment, then took the proffered hand, shaking it firmly. 'I am in your debt, Mr Stedman, for taking care of Jessica at such a traumatic time ...' Then he turned his attention back on her, his expression immediately grim. 'Helen has not yet regained consciousness,' he informed her. 'But the doctors show optimism that she has passed the point of real danger.'

'And Stavros?' she asked anxiously.

The older man's head drooped a little on his straight shoulders. 'He is awake and alert,' he said heavily. 'But he——well, come,' he murmured on an uncharacteristic change of mind. 'We will go and see him—he is out of bed and striding the corridors of the hospital like a man demented. I worry that my son finds his conscience an unbearable burden at this time; perhaps you can help ease his mind somewhat, for I know he is impatient to see you.'

They walked—an odd trio, Jessica flanked either side by two large and lean men—through the quiet hallways of the hospital.

'Stavros has some facial lacerations. I tell you this so you will not be shocked, but they are merely superficial, and it is only his concussion which keeps the doctors on their toes, as he refuses to rest.' Jessica nodded mutely, too tense to speak.

They turned a corner, and Jessica's gaze instantly alighted on the woebegone figure of Stavros Kirilakis slumped over in a chair, his black head buried in his hands. On a soft cry, she rushed forwards, leaving the two other men to watch grimly as she fell to her knees beside her brother-in-law and took him tenderly into her arms.

It was a moving scene, the slender young woman cradling the large Greek to her, while he, in an uncontrolled act of distress, drew her close and pushed his dark head into the sweetly scented mass of pale hair. They remained like that for a while, gaining strength from each other, then Stavros was lifting his head and talking quickly and painfully to Jessica, while she remained kneeling, her hand smoothing his lacerated face, listening, caring, loving, their exchange of words too low to be overheard.

Aristotle Kirilakis touched his companion's arm. 'We intrude, I think,' he said quietly; his glance went briefly to Alec's face, catching a look of pained yearning that made the older man find a small, wry smile. 'Come, Mr Stedman,' he urged. 'I think you and I can go somewhere to drink coffee and discuss your relationship with my son's sister-in-law.'

As they began to turn away, Stavros came wearily to his feet, bringing Jessica with him, and they walked slowly towards the closed door behind which Helen lay so frighteningly ill. They were clinging to each other, the imperious Greek not too proud to lean on the softer strength of the woman holding him so tenderly.

Stavros stood close behind Jessica, his hands resting on her shoulders while hers gripped fiercely at the metal rail at the foot of the bed, her eyes blurred with helpless tears as she looked at Helen lying so pale and still.

A thick white bandage hid her lovely hair from sight and covered one half of her face. An arm was in plaster from wrist to shoulder, the other looking painfully fragile by comparison. A cage held the covers away from her legs, and she knew from what Stavros had just told her outside in the corridor that Helen's legs were badly bruised, though thankfully not broken. But it was the things she couldn't see that threatened Jessica's composure. When Helen had been thrown from the car she had received a severe blow to her midsection, causing damage to her ribs and serious internal bleeding. It had also lost her her baby, the pregnancy too early to allow the premature child any hope. A son. Helen had conceived another son, and she didn't even know about his tragic loss.

'The doctors believe she has stabilised at last,' said Stavros rawly from behind her. 'For a few hours they thought——' He couldn't say it, his voice breaking, and Jessica reached up to cover his resting hand with hers to tell him she understood. 'They don't know how long she will remain unconscious. The bump on her head indicates concussion, but there is no fracture, and they are optimistic that her unconsciousness is just the body's natural way of keeping her at peace while it gets on with the job of healing.'

'She looks so very ill,' Jessica whispered thickly. 'So helpless lying there.'

'But she fights, Jessica,' Stavros stated firmly, sensing her need for reassurance, seeing, with a sensitivity brought on by his own fears, that it was his turn to be strong, and hers to lean. 'She is strong and fearless when fighting for something she wants. You and I both know that. Helen's frailty is as illusory as your own, my dear.'

It was an hour before Jessica left her sister's side, and at her brother-in-law's insistence when he noted that the strain of the anxiety, plus the added stresses of a long journey, were beginning to take their toll on her, and that she was looking as pale and sickly as her poor sister.

When she let herself quietly out of the hospital room, Stavros was sitting on a chair beside his wife, her un-injured hand clasped in his. Jessica took a last look back just before she closed the door. The dark head had lowered to the white sheet, his other hand lying along the pillow just above Helen's bandaged head. He was crying quietly.

Outside in the corridor waited Aristotle Kirilakis—alone.

Jessica looked at him with dull eyes as he came to his feet. 'Where's Alec?' she asked him, immediately aware of his absence.

The older man lifted his hands in a conciliatory gesture. 'He has gone, my dear.' He said it very gently. 'Back to London. Commitments insist he return home once he had assured himself of your safe arrival at your family's side... He is a good man, Jessica, a considerate man. He said to tell you farewell and to take good care of yourself.'

'Gone?' she whispered in a bewildered little voice. 'Alec has gone?'

Aristotle's grave look of sympathy was her undoing. Jessica stared blankly at him for a moment longer. Then she burst into tears.

CHAPTER TWELVE

THE ensuing three days went by in a strange, timeless fashion. Long, long daylight hours of unbearable waiting for news from the hospital that Helen had regained consciousness. The nights—harder to bear because the blessed escape through sleep remained elusive when the imagination, weakened by the severe constraint exerted on it during the day, would run amok with the emotions, leaving Jessica barely fit to begin the next long, frustrating day.

Stavros spent all his time at the hospital with Helen, sitting by her bed, talking to her, worrying, cursing in sharp, brief explosions of pent-up emotion—and slept, fitfully, when they managed to physically force him to lie down in the room next door to Helen's. Between them, Jessica and Aristotle took it in turns to be with him at the hospital, while Mrs Kirilakis took over the mothering of a quietly bewildered Yannis, too young to understand exactly what had happened, but perceptive enough to sense everyone's worry. Though he never enquired, Jessica knew he was aware that his parents' absence from their home was more than just another business trip, and he tended to cling to Jessica when she was at the villa, jealously possessive of her free time.

'It is your likeness to his mama,' Mrs Kirilakis judged sadly. 'He sees his mama in you and so he clings. Children are such sensitive creatures. We tend to forget that in times of trial.'

And through it all, Jessica found herself having to contend with a tumult of confusing feelings over Alec's abrupt desertion. It was as though Helen's brief courting with death had laid bare all those feelings she had so successfully hidden away, and she no longer knew what

154

she wanted or even needed from him—she only knew that his going had left an empty space inside her that she found difficult to cope with.

Helen woke up the next day.

Jessica was with her, sitting in the chair beside the bed, talking quietly to the unaware woman, telling her all her troubles, spilling out her confusing thoughts with an inhibition that was relying on the fact that she would not be overheard, and she had been so lost in her ramblings that she didn't even notice pale lids lift and blue eyes turn in her direction. It was the sound of a feeble voice that pulled her out of her self-absorption.

'Jess, what are you doing here?'

'Helen!' Jessica jumped to her feet, the strain on her face breaking up with a wavering smile as she came to lean over her sister. 'Helen,' she said again tearfully, and kissed the smooth, pale cheek left unbandaged.

'Where am I? What happened?' Her uninjured hand went to her bandaged head, her confusion evident in the weary strain in her eyes. 'Wh-where is Stavros? Jess——!' The hand came to clutch at Jessica's arm, instant recall evident in the sudden and blinding fear that shot into her eyes. 'Where is...'

'He's fine!' Jessica rushed to reassure. 'Fine, darling. He's sleeping, next door. We've all been very worried about you, and getting him to rest has been a battle worthy of a medal, but Stavros is fine.' If 'fine' covered the state of the haggard man lying in an exhausted sleep, she added grimly to herself. In his own way, Stavros looked in worse shape than Helen.

'We—crashed,' her sister mumbled, struggling to remember.

'Yes, darling,' Jessica said gently, her hand going surreptitiously for the call button above the bed, worried because she could see that Helen was already making a detailed inventory of her injuries. She was going to ask the inevitable any moment now, and Jessica knew that was one question she didn't relish answering. 'Four days ago.' She threw in the red herring with a silent prayer that it would divert Helen.

It did; her eyes widened with surprise. 'Four days?' she whispered hoarsely. 'I've been lying here for four days?'

'Yes.' Jessica managed a teasing smile. 'How lazy can you get?'

Helen relaxed back on the pillows, closing her eyes for a moment, running her tongue across dry lips, and Jessica gave the call button another vicious stab, worriedly watching her Helen go very pale again.

'A drink of water,' she whispered.

'Of course,' Jessica replied, contritely, because she should have thought of that herself. She straightened away from the bed to reach for the Thermos flask of cool water, pouring some into a glass.

'I've lost the baby, haven't I.' It wasn't a question, but a quiet statement of fact.

Jessica's hand shook. 'Yes, darling,' she replied heavily. 'I'm so very sorry.'

She moved back to the bed, leaning over to slip an arm beneath her sister's shoulders and lifting her enough for her to sip from the glass. Helen dutifully complied, no sign of distress apparent, and Jessica was about to heave on an inner sigh of relief when Helen lifted her eyes up to hers, and her heart squeezed painfully at the look of abject misery mirrored there.

'Jess——' she said weakly, 'w-would you get Stavros for m-me?'

Jessica gently laid her back on the pillows, unable to hide her emotional reaction to that broken little request. 'Right away, darling.' She kissed Helen's cheek again and got up, her limbs like jelly beneath her, the need to just break down and cry almost overwhelming as she moved quickly towards the door.

Stavros was fast asleep, lying fully clothed on the top of the stark hospital bed, black hair ruffled, face white beneath his natural tan, and still showing the scars of his own injuries. Jess moved silently to the bed and touched his shoulder gently.

He came awake with a jerk, black eyes flicking open to stare red-rimmed but alert at Jessica.

'Helen is awake,' she said levelly.

He came off the bed in a single reflex action, standing swaying beside Jessica, a hand rubbing harshly at his face. 'I must go to her——'

'Stavros...' Jessica stalled him as he moved towards the door, eyes showing her inner sorrow. 'She—she knows.'

His haggard face closed, shoulders stooping for the moment it took him to recover from the blow that dealt him, then he was straightening and moving with his old lithe grace out of the room.

Jessica rang Teddy a week after her rushed exit from London.

'How long are you going to be away?' was his first question, once she'd given a brief account of events.

'How long have they given me?' she came back wryly.

'Two weeks,' Teddy told her. 'And reluctantly, at that. You want to thank your lucky stars, sweetie, that your understudy wasn't up to standard,' he trilled ruefully. 'But, as it is—I could probably swing you another week if the lady requires it.'

Jessica understood exactly what he was getting at. If her stand-in had been worthy, Jessica would have been out. Theatre actors were not supposed to have personal problems when working, they were supposed to restrict those kinds of disruptions for when they were 'resting'. She had, in effect, broken her contract by leaving the play, and they were within their legal rights to replace her permanently.

They chatted for a while longer, Jess catching up on the London news and Teddy more than willing to relay all the juicy bits of theatre gossip, then, when he paused for a rare breath, Jessica inserted as casually as she could make it, 'Have you seen anything of Aunty Vi?'

She hated herself for being so desperate for news of Alec. But ever since he'd turned up at her flat she hadn't been able to get him out of her mind. His quick departure from the hospital had wounded her. He had been so much like the man she first fell in love with during that long and traumatic journey, kind and considerate, there purely to make things as easy for her as he could. Then—gone. No word other than that totally unsatisfying message left with Aristotle, leaving her feeling bereft all over again.

There was a short silence, then Teddy said in that odd way people use when they assume you know something you don't, 'She's in Devon—Alec sent her off with a couple of her old cronies for a holiday while he was away. You know she hates staying alone in that big house, sweetie! So The Man booked four of them into a hotel and left it to *moi* to transport them all down there— didn't the naughty man tell you about it?' Teddy went on curiously. 'I must presume that he will return to London with you, since he wrote old Teddy out a list as long as your pretty arm of people I had to contact to cancel his appointments for the next month—wish I could drift off for a month like that,' he went on grumpily while Jessica tried to make some sense of what Teddy was saying. It sounded as though—no, she decided, she was reading things into his words that weren't there! Wishful thinking, Jess! she damned herself. Alec couldn't possibly still be on——

'I—I haven't seen Alec since we arrived here a week ago,' she put in guardedly.

'No?' Teddy sounded decidedly puzzled. 'Funny,' he mused. 'Got a postcard off him only yesterday, said he was drowning in history, said his camera had gone into overdrive taking pics, said he was thinking of changing his theme and going in for historical monuments instead of faces, said he...'

'He's still here!' Jessica whispered breathlessly, a slither of excitement running through her.

'Mentioned that brother-in-law of yours,' Teddy confirmed glibly. 'Borrowing his boat, he said, thinking of taking it around the island.'

Stavros knew Alec was here! Jessica stood like a woman pole-axed, unable to make head nor tail of the whole puzzle.

'He said...'

'Goodbye, Teddy,' Jessica cut in absently. 'I'll call you again when I can give you a firm date for my return.' And she put down the phone, shaking like a leaf, her mind flying off in all directions, alternately feeling surprise, delight, anger, suspicion, and a shocking excitement that held her in that baffled daze until Mrs Kirilakis came up to tap her shoulder, making her jump.

'You are all right, Jessica?' she enquired curiously, her tall frame still straight and elegant, revealing a beauty that must have been devastating in her youth.

'I—I think so...' she replied uncertainly, still staring blankly outwards. 'I—I...' She dragged herself together. 'Do you think Yannis will be very upset if I sneak out for an hour or so? I need to speak to Stavros.'

'I'm sure he won't mind,' came the calming reply. Yannis had made Jessica his surrogate mother, and hardly let her out of his sight when his father wasn't around to be with him. But Jessica had a glint in her eyes that the older woman had not seen before; it was as if someone had turned on a light inside her, and Mrs Kirilakis would do anything to keep it shining there. 'He's with his grandfather now, fishing off the end of the jetty. Why don't you run off now? Take the car—and drive carefully, Jessica!' she called after her as Jessica spun and made a flying escape for the door, her heart pounding in her breast, eyes alight with an energy that hadn't been evident since she heard of her sister's accident.

It took nearly an hour to reach Rhodes Town by car, the heavy tourist traffic a constant stream all the way there. This was one of the reasons Stavros usually travelled into the town by boat; it might not be much quicker, but it was certainly pleasanter. Jessica wound her way down past the old town, the beautiful harbour on her other side packed with sailing-boats and fishing-boats alike, the Greek sun blazing relentlessly down, glinting off polished brass and bright white paintwork, reflecting off the crystal-clear water, people walking leisurely around in the least clothes possible, all deeply tanned, looking as if the sun had entered right into their bodies and was shining back out again through their contented faces.

She parked close by the hospital and walked the rest of the way, alive to things she hadn't noticed since arriving on her beloved Rhodes: the heat on her receptive skin, the sun on her pale hair, the spring in her step as she walked, and the excited rush of her blood through her veins. I've come alive, she thought dazedly. Alec is still here on Rhodes and I've come alive!

But by the time she entered her sister's private room the excitement had changed to wariness, Alec's puzzling motives bringing back all those defences she had built up against him over the last months, and she appeared the usual Jessica when she went over to kiss Helen's cheek.

'What are you doing here today?' Helen wanted to know, pleased none the less to see her. Stavros was half sitting, half reclining on the bed beside his wife, looking lazily unconcerned about the intimacy of the scene.

'I wanted to borrow your husband, since you don't need him while you're lying there being so lazy,' Jessica said teasingly.

Helen glared sternly at her. 'Get your own man!' she advised in mock defiance. 'This one's taken.' Her hand went to clasp possessively at the large brown one close by, and Stavros grinned smugly, lifting hers to his lips to present it with a kiss, enjoying this mock battle over his favours.

Helen was looking so much better. The bandage had gone from her head, and the bruising had mellowed to an ugly but less painful yellowy blue. She still couldn't put any weight on her bruised legs, and her arm would be in plaster for some weeks to come, but she looked more the darling sister Jessica adored, only that shadow in her soft blue eyes giving any hint of the deeper inner mourning she was suffering for the loss of her baby.

At first, both she and Stavros had been inconsolable, clinging together in their grief. But slowly, as the days had passed, and a natural acceptance of things one has no control over began to sink in, they had begun to look outwards again. The fact that the child Stavros swerved to avoid when the accident occurred was only alive because of his quick reaction was a kind of balm, although, if he were given the choice between his own child's life and another's his decision would bear no analysing. It would be unfair to try. Helen had said to Jessica only the day before that the fates had ways of making these unenviable choices for us, and in that they had to be grateful.

'Who drove you here, Jessica *mou*?' Stavros put in with a laziness that didn't reflect in the narrowing of his eyes.

'I drove myself!' Jessica pouted, flashing her own brand of arrogance back at him because she knew what was on his mind. He had become manic about car-driving since the accident. Neither Jessica nor his mother had been allowed behind a car wheel, and until now they had complied with his wishes because they hadn't wanted to add to his worries. 'I had this—uncontrollable desire to steal you away from my sister, and I just climbed in the Mercedes and drove!'

'Lunch?' he queried, leaving the other complaint alone for the moment, his eyes still narrowed calculatingly on Jessica's overbright face.

She nodded eagerly. 'At that nice taverna by Mandraki Harbour.' The tables there spilled out across the lawns right down to the harbour wall itself, with gaily patterned umbrellas to keep off the heat of the sun.

'I want to come,' complained Helen, sighing wistfully.

'Well, you can't,' said Jessica firmly, playing the femme fatale game to the hilt. 'I need a man, and only one will do. You've monopolised him enough.'

'I *own* him!' Helen pointed out, trying not to laugh.

'My dear...' Stavros drawled, putting in his own fourpence worth. 'No one "owns" me.'

Helen turned glinting blue eyes on him, their faces mere inches apart. 'Really?' she challenged softly.

He gazed darkly back at her, and Jessica fondly watched his features soften and take on a whole new expression. She, too, had noticed the brief disappearance of pain from Helen's eyes.

'I promise to bring him back when I've finished with him,' Jessica put in helpfully.

'Oh—well——' her sister conceded, 'in that case...'

They decided to walk the short distance to the harbour, Jessica becoming abstracted the moment they stepped out into the sunshine. Stavros made no comment, but his face wore a considering look as he walked beside her.

Stavros was well known on the island, and his car accident had caused a mild sensation with the native Rhodians, so their progress to the harbour was a slow one, Stavros having to stop often to receive condolences and good wishes for his lovely wife in quick-fire Greek that left Jessica lost from the moment it began. The islanders' warmth of heart and physical demonstration of such in man-to-man embraces and sympathetic slaps on the back were a pleasure to witness. And the way Stavros joined in the easy friendliness made her uncomfortably aware of the English lack of the same.

By the time they arrived at the taverna, Jessica was smiling wryly at the amount of times their progress had been halted. 'I bet you're black and blue,' she teased as they sat down at a table set slightly apart from the others. It had taken Stavros just two minutes to have it placed where he wanted it, the owner coming out personally to shake hands with his honoured visitor, their booming voices carrying across the café to make heads turn in curious appreciation. It took little discernment to see that Stavros was thought of as someone special in these parts. His bearing alone stated as much, yet no one could criticise his natural Greek friendliness, nor his open consideration for his beautiful young companion.

'We are an honest and naturally open-hearted people, Jessica,' he informed her with just a small touch of hauteur to show her that he did not take kindly to derision when it was aimed at his beloved Rhodian people. 'Look around you and see how your English counterparts clutch fearfully at their purses in case of robbery, yet here they could walk away and leave their precious possessions sitting in open view on the table-top and I could almost guarantee that no stone would be left unturned in an effort to return them to their rightful owner. We haven't even a jail here, did you know?' Grimness made way for a smile at her surprised expression. 'If our police do have cause to lock someone up, they have to be transported by hydrofoil to Kos! Take my advice,' he added with finger-wagging mockery, 'and don't become drunk and disorderly, or it could cost you the price of a ticket to Kos, plus the inconvenience of a short jail stay.'

'You're ribbing me!' she derided accusingly.

Stavros went all Greek on her. 'Ribbing? What is this ribbing? Ribs are things which protect the heart from danger; they are the slender, curving bones my dear Helen has bandaged tightly beneath her pretty nightgown.'

Jessica looked suspiciously at him, unsure whether or not he was teasing her. The trouble with foreigners, she decided poutingly, deliberately disregarding the fact that she was the foreigner at this particular table, was that you couldn't tell whether they were pulling your leg or genuinely serious!

'I'll have one of those wonderful salads you Greeks are famous for.' Being uncertain of her ground in the other subject, she turned the conversation to food.

'You'll have what Nikos serves us,' Stavros warned firmly. 'Or prepare yourself for a display of outraged Greek sensibilities!'

What actually arrived was a dream of a thick, juicy lamb steak, served with a delicious, lightly seasoned sauce and crisp par-cooked vegetables, followed by the naughtiest sweet she had ever seen! Layers of sliced peaches picked fresh from the tree, big juicy strawberries sandwiched between ice cream, with generous whips of fresh cream on top, topped with fresh cherries.

It was a delight and a challenge. 'I won't eat all that!' Jessica gasped.

'No?' quizzed Stavros, clearly not believing her.

He was right and she was wrong, and he was still laughing at her when she sat back bloated in her seat, staring mulishly at him. 'You are an evil devil, Stavros Kirilakis,' she accused. 'I brought you out for a pleasant "light" lunch, and you feed me up as if preparing me for slaughter!'

He sat back, the smile still playing on his lips, but when he lifted his gaze to hers, it was quite serious. 'Perhaps now you will tell me, my dear Jessica, why you dragged me away from my dear wife's sick-bed, hmm?'

Jessica lost her sense of humour too, her gaze drifting to the harbour and the hundreds of bobbing crafts lining the sun-drenched wall.

Now she had his full attention, she wasn't sure just what she required from him. Surely, she argued with herself, if Alec was still on the island, then the fact that he hadn't even tried to contact her was a message in itself—wasn't it? Which left her in two minds whether or not to bring him up at all.

'I do believe that, if you sat here long enough, everyone on Rhodes would pass by you eventually,' she murmured absently, her skin shining with the sunkissed glow where the huge umbrella above their heads didn't quite shade her. Her simple dress of lemon cotton complemented her delicate fairness.

'And would you consider sitting here if you believed one person in particular might do just that and pass by your table?'

Shrewd as ever, Stavros hit the nail right on the head and made no real bones about it. Jessica turned to view him solemnly. Did anything ever get by him without his being aware of it? She thought not.

She took in a deep breath and let it out again slowly, dropping her eyes to the cleared table in between them. 'When you consider all the complications which could have arisen from the accident, Helen is—lucky to still be able to bear you more children once she is well enough.'

A flicker of pain crossed his face. The doctors had only yesterday confirmed that Helen was in no way damaged internally as a result of the violent loss of their child.

'You are—concerned for her, my dear?' His voice automatically deepened into gentleness; Stavros was well aware how close the two sisters were. He was also aware that Jessica had just deftly steered the subject off in another direction.

She sighed pensively. 'Only for a while—as we all were. No,' she said dully. 'I was making a selfish comparison that has little to do with Helen,' she admitted on a grimace. 'Alec's wife must have been utterly crushed when her—admittedly deliberate abortion ruined her chances of ever having children again. I feel—uncomfortable, because it has taken Helen's situation to bring that point firmly home to me...I can now understand why Alec was so concerned for Tracy.'

'What are you trying to say, Jessica?' Stavros probed carefully. 'That you now rue the way you sent him away without giving him a hearing?'

'I gave him a hearing, Stavros,' she stated curtly, instantly on the defensive. 'And, even with a new view of his dilemma then, it doesn't alter the fact that he chose Tracy above me. I have feelings too, you know! And I won't come second in line to any woman!'

Stavros took his time answering that, seemingly intent on following the line of bobbing sailing-boats tied up at the quay before he turned to catch Jessica's gaze with hooded eyes.

'Do you recall, dear, when I visited you in London and we discussed the subject matter of your play?'

She nodded. 'The absurdity of arranged marriages,' she said.

'We—we touched on my own problems in facing a similar situation within my own old-fashioned family.'

'Your parents adore Helen now, and you know it,' she put it wryly. 'I am absolutely certain they wouldn't want to swap her for the girl they originally chose for you.'

'You are entirely correct,' he agreed. 'But that isn't the point I am trying to make.' He paused, gathering his thoughts, then sat forward, arms resting easily on the table-top. 'The young woman in question—Ianthe—had grown from childhood expecting to become my wife eventually. I was, to her indoctrinated mind, her property. Yet, do you know, she didn't even like me!' Stavros shook his head ruefully. 'I was too strong a person in my own right for Ianthe. She needed a man she could rule; her own nature is not so far removed from my own, so we clashed continuously and on every level, but, when Helen came on the scene and she saw her possession being taken away from her, she fought to keep hold of it with every weapon she had available. It didn't matter to her that I wasn't the right man for her, nor that I was determined never to marry her no matter what. She set out to ruin things between Helen and me—and almost succeeded,' he admitted grimly. 'If it hadn't been for—certain circumstances coming to my attention, Helen and I would never have married. I came to my senses soon enough to come after Helen when she'd run away from me back to England, and beg her forgiveness for believing the lies that had been fed to me. But . . .'

'You cannot be comparing your situation then with Alec and his ex-wife!' Jessica disclaimed. 'For a start,

Tracy Lopez didn't need to lie and cheat to get Alec eating out of her pretty little hand, she only had to play on his overactive conscience!' She gets to me, Alec had said.

'But do you know for sure that she did not lie and cheat and use every tactic available to her to stop Alec from marrying you?'

'He never offered me marriage,' she pointed out tightly.

'But your affair was well publicised, and maybe she feared a marriage in the offing and so the end of her hold over Alec.' He let that sink in for a moment, then went on carefully, 'You know, Jessica, that Christhanson pride has a terrible lack of forgiveness attached to it. Have you ever allowed Alec the opportunity to explain why he never carried out his intentions and remarried his ex-wife?'

'Maybe he no longer wants to explain,' Jessica suggested offhandedly, still hurting from his defection on their arrival on the island. 'He's here, isn't he?' she challenged, blue eyes angry on her brother-in-law. 'Enjoying a pleasant vacation on this island somewhere, and not in the least concerned about seeing me at all!'

'Ah!' said Stavros, satisfied, her flash of anger telling him everything he wanted to know. 'But if he happened to walk past this table in the next minute and offered to explain, you would maybe, at last, be willing to listen?'

Jessica shrugged evasively. She had the feeling she was being led somewhere she didn't want to go; Stavros was good at that, setting nice soft traps for you to fall into.

'Maybe,' she murmured warily. 'If Alec wanted to—talk things over—I would be prepared to listen now, yes.'

'And you will acknowledge that you may just owe him that chance?' persisted a man who saw some kind of victory in sight.

'Owe?' She picked up on the word and scorned it. 'I owe Alec nothing.'

'Time, Jessica *mou*, you owe him time,' Stavros stated gently. 'Alec gave up his time to bring you safely to us when we needed you, and that kind of debt, by Greek law, must be repaid.'

'But if I don't know where he is I can't give back his damned time, can I?' she said sarcastically, so much on the defensive that Stavros smiled.

'Who told you Alec was still on the island?'

'Teddy,' she snapped. 'I spoke to Teddy this morning on the phone, he—he happened to mention it.'

'And you immediately came running to find me because your eagerness to know where Alec is outrode that stubborn pride of yours,' Stavros finished for her on a low, aggravating laugh.

'Teddy said something about Alec borrowing your boat, so I presumed you must know he was here,' she admitted sullenly.

'And if I do have that kind of information, what will you do with it if I pass it on to you?'

Jessica gazed out at the harbour with a sullen mutiny written on her face. Then she turned back to face her brother-in-law.

'I think—if Alec is here, I would probably go and search him out.'

'Why?' Stavros demanded softly.

'Why?' she echoed, and all at once the defiance left her, leaving in its wake only a painfully vulnerable woman. 'Because—because I need him. Because I w-want him.' Her pretty blue eyes filled with weak tears, and she added on a quivering murmur, 'Because I love him.'

A spasm of remorse rippled across her ruthless inter-rogator's face, and his hand came out to press hers in apology.

'Where is he, Stavros?' Jessica asked on a thin whisper.

His eyes were black in the brooding grimness of his face. The hot sun beat down, etching out a clean circle of shadow around the two of them, and Jessica waited, breathing suspended, while Stavros seemed to do silent battle with himself. He shook his head and sighed in heavy dissatisfaction.

'I can't tell you, my dear,' he said at last, and watched, with a tightening of his jaw, her fine lids lower to hide her disappointment. 'The last time I spoke to him, he was considering taking the hydrofoil over to Kos and spending a few days visiting the tourist spots over there. But I will make enquiries, Jessica,' he promised firmly, urging her to trust him. 'And when I find your Alec, you may be sure that you will be the first to know.'

CHAPTER THIRTEEN

BUT when Alec did come, he took her so much by surprise that she forgot all about promising to listen to him, and shock and anger had her spitting more insults at him than she knew herself capable of!

It was very early the next morning when, after a night of restless tossing and turning, Jess had got up, pulled on a pair of shorts and a skimpy T-shirt and, as had become her habit since arriving at the villa, had gone silently outside before anyone else was awake.

The private bay looked wonderful at this time of the morning. Beneath her bare feet, the sand felt hot even at this early hour. The sea swished lazily against the shoreline, drawing her down towards its edge, making her catch her breath at that first touch of clean, cold water to her warm toes. She stood there for a while, looking about her with a feeling of deep inner contentment.

Stavros had come home by sea the night before, and the yacht swayed gently on its rope moorings, tied to the natural jetty cut by nature like an outstretched finger into the bay. The yacht was half in darkness, her bow glinting bright white in the sunlight, her stern lost in the shadow of the steep cliff-face. The water was very deep there, which allowed for the boat to come in so close to land, and so crystal-clear that Jessica and Yannis would spend hours just sitting, feet dangling over the side of the jetty, watching the varied marine life carrying on its own way of life beneath the surface.

This morning the air was very still; barely a breeze disturbed the tranquillity of the bay, and Jessica lingered to enjoy the peace, catching with a smile the leap of an over-eager fish out in the middle of the bay. A large bird flew silently overhead, and Jessica tipped her head up to watch it soar on a current of air across the bay from one side to the other, its incredible wing-span making her wonder if it might be one of the eagles that nested on the island. Another splash had her head flicking around and back to the water, searching with squinting eyes for the telltale whirl of water that would show her where the leaping fish had risen this time. She could see no evidence out in the middle of the bay, and began a careful search of the shadowed perimeter, knowing it was a useless search, but doing it anyway, just enjoying the wonderful simplicity in having nothing more to do than watch and listen and absorb and feel.

It was then she saw it, moving with a golden grace through the water, coming out of the shadows from the direction of the yacht, and out into the bright sunlight, striking out an oblique line towards her.

A man! she recognised with a flutter of alarm; it was most certainly a man swimming towards the beach from the direction of the yacht. Had Stavros unwittingly brought a stowaway home with him last night? It seemed a remarkable notion if he had. The yacht was only big enough for day-sailing in relative comfort. She had a cabin, but it was small and geared to eating the odd light lunch in, its narrow bench-seat not big enough to even stretch out on if you wanted to sleep.

He came out of the water like Helios rising, water streaming from his shoulders and down his magnificent golden frame. His hair, tawny streaked with gold, was flattened to the proud shape of his head, eyes of a hunting lion fixed on her mesmerised figure, and Jessica's breath caught in her throat, seeing him as she had once imagined seeing him. Her Colossus rising from his watery resting place to come for her. Her heart responded violently, hammering in her breast.

'Alec,' she breathed tremulously.

He said nothing, but just kept coming, his square chin set in a stubborn line, an air of purpose about him that had Jessica taking jerky steps backwards the closer he came.

'W-what are you doing here?'

If she expected the question to stall him, then she was quickly disabused of that idea. He didn't even falter. Up he came, his thighs now free of the glistening water, white swimming trunks so brief they left little to the imagination, knees solid and sure, calves thick and firmly muscled. He kept moving, the water splashing around his bare feet.

Jess giggled, not with amusement at this novel appearance, but more a high-pitched, nervous giggle because he looked so big, so determined and very, very grim.

'You—you——' She was backing up as he came, hands held out in front of her, trying desperately to appear at ease, while inside she was a mass of confusion and alarm. 'You s-slept on the y-yacht last night?'

No reply. He reached her, stopped, looming over her like some mystical, avenging giant. Those narrowed lion eyes held hers for a moment, giving her only the briefest hint as to what he intended to do before he bent and, with a smooth ease that infuriated her, picked her up and threw her over his shoulder. Before she'd even had a chance to take in what was happening, he turned and began walking across the soft, silver sand towards the quay.

'Alec!' she cried, struggling in an effort to get free. 'What are doing? *Alec!*' she repeated angrily when he made no sign that he'd even heard her, walking along, the water still clinging in big round globules to his skin, the coolness of his body acting as a stimulant on her sun-warmed skin. 'Put me down!' she demanded furiously, kicking out with her feet, only to find them deftly caught and clamped against his body, and he continued to walk on as though she were not there. Her lips clamping angrily together, she brought her fists down hard on his solid back, thumping at him, hair dangling all about her face, anger climbing along with indignation at her position.

'Alec——' she warned, finding this not in the least bit funny, the blood beginning to rush to her head. 'If you don't put me down this minute I'll—I'll start screaming!' she warned. 'And the whole household will hear me and come running!'

Try it, his silence challenged. And she did, opening her mouth and emitting a shrill scream which surprised even her! But it was no use. Alec kept up his steady pace, ignoring her completely, and Jessica felt the slow rise of a fearful excitement beginning to curdle her blood. It was alarming, this being carried off by a big, silent man, feeling useless, vulnerable. It didn't matter that she knew him, and knew without doubt that Alec meant her no physical harm, it was the way in which he was doing it, so determined on his set course that he wasn't even listening to her protests.

He was carrying her along the jetty now, getting ever nearer to the bulky darkness where the sun hadn't yet penetrated, making for the yacht, and Jessica began struggling in earnest, frantically trying to wriggle out of his grip, her face hot with anger and humiliation—and too much blood! She screamed again, loud and long, and Alec let go of her legs long enough to issue a stinging slap to her rear.

'Oh!' she cried, mortified. 'I'll kill you for this, Alec Stedman!' she choked, pummelling him with her fists. 'I hate you—hate you!'

He didn't even scorn her with a laugh, but reached the yacht and stepped lithely on to the deck. The boat swayed a little and he paused only long enough to make certain of his balance, then he was going down the steps to the small cabin, sliding her off his shoulder until she was clamped firmly to his body, faces level, eyes revealing different expressions: hers a furious frustration, his a cold determination.

He stepped through the cabin door, let go of her, watched impassively as she whirled angrily away from him and across the cramped room, hair flying out, face flushed dark red and rigid. Then, with a mocking bow that brought an animal growl to her lips, he stepped back outside, closing the door behind him.

'What are you *doing*?' She jumped back to the door in time to hear the bolt slide firmly home on the other side. Her legs went to jelly, and she clutched madly at the doorframe, listening with growing horror to his footsteps calmly taking him back up on deck. 'Alec!' Her fist hit the door, knuckles stinging with the foolish action.

She could hear him walking above her, and her eyes tipped upwards, following him as he moved. There was a pause, when the silence held her breath locked in her throat, then the throaty sound of the engine starting up, and Jessica felt her temper blow.

He was abducting her! she realised furiously—ignoring the tingle of excitement his caveman tactics was stirring in her—that great big arrogant *oaf* had the nerve to think he could—— 'Alec Stedman! You get down here and let me *out*!' she yelled with a childish stamp of a bare foot.

Each time she threw a new threatening command at him, her voice rose up a notch until even she recognised that she was shrieking like the demented, but it didn't stop her yelling abuse at him, nor pummelling the door with an anger she would never have thought herself capable of feeling.

They were moving now, the yacht turning slowly on its axis, engine throbbing sluggishly while the manoeuvre was completed, then she heard the change in tone as Alec opened up the throttle, and they were off, cutting a slanting line towards the narrow exit of the bay.

Jess flung herself at the small porthole, peering out, fingers fumbling agitatedly with the catch so she could throw it open, eyes glittering as they carefully traced the direction the yacht took once beyond the rocky fingers of land, then she was back at the door, flinging herself bodily at it, shouting out yet more insults until, hot and exhausted, she slumped wearily on the bench seat, her body bathed in the sweat of her exertions, throat sore and dry with shouting.

'I'll never forgive you for this!' was her final and most shrill cry. 'You wait until Stavros catches up with you, he'll have my permission to have you castrated!'

In fact, she thought murderously, I may even do it myself!

She got up, went over to the small fridge and peered inside, relieved to find it well stocked with canned drinks.

She selected a Coke for herself, ripping off the seal to guzzle greedily at the refreshing drink. 'I hope you're frying up there,' she muttered, visualising him at the helm, the sun hot on his skin, mouth dry and cracked, and took another deep gulp at the Coke. 'I hope you're pleased with yourself, Alec damned Stedman. I'll get you back,' she muttered on. 'I'll get you back!' She shouted out the angry threat, then subsided back on to the bench seat to await, in a more ladylike manner, her fate.

Later, Jessica couldn't say what had infuriated her the most—his insufferable calmness at the way he had kidnapped her, or the terrible nerve-racking silence he subjected her to. She certainly was not afraid for her life, nor of the actual kidnap itself. In fact, when she looked back later, she'd found that part rather exciting. But, as the minutes ticked by and the boat still continued on its course around the island, and the silence from the man steering them remained firm, she learned to know the meaning of the phrase 'a mental fraying', because it happened to her.

She was sitting quietly on the bench seat when the yacht eventually came to a halt. The engine shivered into silence, and she heard the sound of the anchor being lowered, then Alec was coming down the steps and unlocking the door.

He still had that no-nonsense look about him, Jessica noted with a nervous quivering inside. His body, still dressed in nothing but those shocking trunks, filled the gap in the doorway with an imperiousness that said the ordeal was not yet over. 'Come on,' he ordered curtly, wafting a hand at her to make her jump to his command. 'Out you come.'

'So, it does speak then?' she sneered, refusing to comply, chin up in mutiny. 'Go to hell,' she added coldly.

He was over at her side so quickly that Jessica jumped, a startled gasp escaping her lips as his hands landed on her shoulders and rudely drew her to her feet.

'It speaks!' he acknowledged harshly. 'And it's been in hell for so long now, it knows no different—so don't rile me any more than you believe you can cope with, Jess,' he warned, 'because this particular Colossus may have been brought to his knees for a time but, unlike the other one, he's up and fighting again. So I'd keep that vicious tongue of yours sweet if I were you, or else know the consequences.'

'Who gave you the right to——'

'Out!' He cut in harshly, pointing imperiously towards the open door. 'Out!'

And Jessica went, too afraid of a repeat performance of his newly acquired strong-arm tactics to defy him any longer. But she threw him a withering look before she moved, tossing her head back in a haughty manner and smiling gleefully to herself when he received a slap from her flying hair, right in his arrogant face.

The sun was getting hotter as it rose higher in the sky, and Jessica came out on top to feel its heat burn her skin, its brilliance making her screw up her eyes while she became used to it. He had anchored them in the mouth of a tiny, sunkissed bay, the circling cliff a face of sheer, unattainable rock, the beach little more than a postage-stamp size of pure white sand.

'Right,' said that authoritative voice from behind her, making her jump and scuttle quickly to the side of the boat, clutching nervously at the rail. She turned in time to see his grim look of satisfaction at her healthy wariness in him. 'Now, I'm going to do the talking and you're going to do the listening, Jess. Got that?'

She nodded, swallowing.

He nodded too, standing a good few feet away from her, yet still close enough to intimidate with his superior size. 'I want to explain about Tracy. She...'

'No!' The negative shot from her without her being able to stop it.

His gaze on her narrowed threateningly. 'I thought we agreed that you...'

'Yes, but—I don't want to hear about your ex-wife,' she told him quickly. 'Just tell me one thing; the rest can stay unsaid for all I'm interested in it.'

He hesitated indecisively. He knew as well as she did that she was in no position to make demands, then he nodded grimly. 'OK—fire away,' he allowed briskly.

'Are you here because your—your feelings for me proved stronger than your sense of duty towards Tracy Lopez, or because she rejected you?'

He was studying her from beneath frowning brows, skin glowing three shades darker than she remembered it to be, the sunshine glinting on the layers of fine body hair that covered his skin, framing him in a haze of pure spun gold.

Magical, mystical, she thought breathlessly, and the desire to run to him and throw herself at his feet made her quiver. Then he smiled, and it was such an odd, twisting, self-mocking smile that it held her trapped against the rail with its impact.

'I knew which was more important to me even as you walked out of the drawing-room that day,' he admitted heavily. A hand lifted emptily towards her, then dropped again, and the smile wavered and died. 'I never—*ever*—want to go through an hour like the one which followed that scene!' he told her roughly, and Jessica watched some of the colour leave his face. 'I had to watch you bleeding to death in front of me, and I couldn't do a damned thing to stop it! I stood there and watched you pack, watched you carefully remove every single item that belonged to you until you'd stripped the place clean of——' his voice broke, and he had to clear his throat before he could go on '—of any evidence that you had ever been there at all, and I wanted to go down on my knees to beg your forgiveness.'

'Then why didn't you?'

'It was too late, wasn't it?' he said bleakly. 'It was too late from the moment I let Tracy get to me with her——'

'I asked you not to speak about her,' Jessica cut in, and knew the venom she felt towards the other woman showed in her voice. 'I'm not one of those women who enjoys knowing she comes second in anything, Alec, so be warned, if you want this to proceed from here on, I won't have your ex-wife's name rammed down my throat!'

A muscle jerked in his jaw. 'OK, I can accept that,' he agreed, understanding more than she realised. The old Jessica wouldn't have felt so vindictive towards another human being. He had placed those feelings inside her, when he had unwittingly used Tracy as a weapon to hurt her, and the knowledge did not sit easily on him. 'Let me just say that I came to my senses too late to do anything to save us from the disastrous course I'd stupidly set us on.'

'Did you try?' she attacked quite ruthlessly.

'Oh, yes, I tried.' His mouth twisted in bitterness. 'Although, I have to say, your slaying of me at the restaurant was a kind of revenge for you—and a lot more public, wasn't it, Jess?' His mouth went awry again, and she had the grace to blush. That particular scene had been juicy enough to warrant reporting in the papers, and Alec hadn't come out looking very good. 'I decided, after that,' he went on grimly, 'that it was no use me trying again, because you obviously had no room in your heart for forgiveness—and I have my pride, too, you know.'

Yes, she knew. 'Then what are you doing here,' she asked tightly, 'if you believe it useless?'

'Ah—this situation is different,' he drawled, relaxing a little at last. 'You asked to see me, if you remember, Jess.'

So she had. She'd forgotten all about that in the shock of his crude way of getting her on this boat, and she shifted uncomfortably under his sharp, challenging gaze.

'Why the caveman tactics?' she threw at him, blue eyes fixed defiantly on him.

His smile came out, brows rising upwards to give his face a devilish charm. 'It did the job, didn't it?' he mocked. 'Got you where I wanted you with the least effort needed—and understand this, Jess,' he went on, irritating her by wagging a finger at her. 'That was only an example of how I mean to continue from now on. The trouble with you is, you live in a world of fantasy make-believe. It's no wonder you're so successful in the profession you chose; having a crazy imagination like yours must be a great asset. But it plays havoc with the mere mortals who try to get close to you. So this one,' he turned that wagging finger on himself, ignoring the way she had stiffened at his critical remarks about her character, 'decided to climb in there with you, since I could see no other way of reaching you—so, here he stands,' he announced with an aggravating mockery of a bow. 'Your Colossus risen. And you're about to learn, Miss Christhanson, that we gods take no messing around

from our temperamental women-folk. You toe the line
or I get tough. It really is as simple as that.'

Jessica stood, amazed at his arrogance, shocked by
his preposterous reading of her, and seething at his pre-
sumption that she would just fall in line with his dic-
tatorial demands!

'God—if I were a man...' she breathed angrily, breasts
heaving up and down beneath the thin cotton T-shirt.

'Wishing you had your Greek brother-in-law with you,
Jess?' he taunted.

'Stavros would throw you overboard if he knew how
you'd treated me today!' she flared.

'Stavros, my dear Jessica,' he drawled silkily, 'helped
me set this whole thing up!'

That did it, knocked all the wind right out of her as
she stared in open-mouthed outrage. They're all the
same, men! she decided furiously. All traitors when put
to the test! She shook her head in disgust, and Alec just
smiled smugly back, so relaxed now that he looked in-
dolent, careless almost, eyeing her with interest as she
jerked from one stage of fury to another until on a low
growl she flew at him, intending to inflict as many
wounds with her nails as she could land before he could
subdue her with his superior strength.

Alec went one better than that. He simply caught her
up as she arrived in front of him, lifted her up high and
quite calmly threw her over the side of the yacht so she
landed in a gurgle of foaming blue ocean, to sink slowly
to the bottom before she gathered her senses enough to
begin swimming back to the surface.

She reappeared, spluttering, to find him leaning casually over the rail, grinning at her like a Cheshire cat.
'You can swim, can't you, Jess?' he asked as a mere
aside.

Swim! she fumed silently, I'll show him how I swim!
With a neatly executed roll, she turned and dived below
the surface, striking out for the beach and swimming
underwater for over a minute before coming back up for
air. By then she was over half-way to the beach, and she
struck out with a crawl that did more to ease her temper
than to show her grace in water.

He was keeping pace with her before she'd reached
the shallows, and she threw him a look meant to drown.
It didn't work. As Alec had said, he'd joined the rule
of gods; he was indestructible.

His hands came around her waist to help her to her
feet in the shallows, holding on to her while she fought
for breath, breathing heavily himself, water streaming
off his near-naked frame, and making her clothes cling
slickly to her body so her skin showed honey-gold against
the sodden cotton.

There was an urgency in his expression that put her
on the attack again. His yellow eyes were glittering
strangely, a streak of red passion glowing along his taut
cheekbones.

'I h-hate y-you, Alec St-Stedman!' she panted angrily.
'You're nothing but an overgrown...'

The rest of her volley was cut off by a warm, moist
mouth covering her own. His arms closed surely around
her, hands splaying her spine to arch her body close to
muscled hardness of his, and Jessica was lost.

Her surrender was that quick, her hungry senses so
desperate for the taste and feel of him that they rushed
through her, burning a trail in their urgency to know
again their perfect match.

'You don't hate me, Jess,' he murmured huskily
against her kiss-softened mouth. 'You love me. You
know you do.'

'No!' she denied, trying again to break free of him.

'Yes!' he insisted harshly, his head coming up so he could glare down at her. 'You love me! You always have done, and even if we never lay eyes on each other again after today, you always will love me!'

He was so, so right! she acknowledged painfully. Tears filled her eyes, and Alec watched them come, his jaw rigid, refusing to give an inch until he had got from her that damning declaration. 'Say it, Jess,' he ordered thickly, giving her an urgent shake. 'Say it, for God's sake, and put us both out of our misery!'

'I love you!' she choked, and dropped her face into his shoulder to cry her heart out.

Alec folded her close, his head dropping gently on to the top of hers, and his big body trembled. 'Marry me, Jess?' he asked roughly.

She made no reply, pushing her face further into his chest.

'Marry me,' he urged again. 'And let me spend a lifetime proving to you how much I love you.'

'Until Tracy shows up again,' she sniffed, clinging to him.

Alec sighed heavily. 'Tracy is no longer my responsibility, Jess. I learned that painful lesson the last time you taught it to me. I don't usually need teaching the same lesson twice.'

'How can I be sure of that?'

'You said you didn't want to hear about Tracy,' he reminded her huskily.

Jessica moved away from him a little and he let her go. The water lapped her knees, cool on her heated skin. 'Tell me,' she mumbled, reluctant even now to hear the other girl's name mentioned.

'I told her, in no uncertain terms, to get the hell out of my life—and she went,' he said bluntly. His hands came up to lightly clasp her wrists, running in a gentle caress upwards to her shoulders. Jessica kept her face averted from him. 'But not before she told me that she'd spun me a pack of lies. The bitch had had herself sterilised at the same time as she had her abortion. Her Italian didn't want to marry her, he'd just thrown her out when he got tired of her. She read about you and me in the paper, saw a possible lifetime meal ticket getting away from her, and decided to come and shove a spoke in the wheel. And that,' he sighed, 'is the sum total, if edited, version of my last conversation with her. She won't bother me again.' His palms absently moulded the rounded bones in Jessica's shoulders. 'I—I have to tell you, Jess,' he added hesitantly, 'that I still couldn't just cut her loose with nothing... I've set her up with a shop, in New York—a classy boutique I'd heard was coming on the market. The last I heard, she was enjoying every minute of it, making a big success of the business, drawing in the wealthy punters like the Pied Piper... If there's one thing you have to admit about her, its her unerring eye for style.'

'OK, we'll give her that,' Jess said, and lifted her face up to smile a watery smile at him.

Her eyes were still red-rimmed from crying, tears glistening on the tips of her lashes, and a sigh shivered through his big body as he lowered his head to brush them away with the feather touch of his lips.

'You know how I hate to see you cry, Jess,' he whispered. 'Why don't you give in and say you'll marry me? There will be no reason for you to cry again then.'

'Arrogant devil,' she rebuked, but her smile was clear at last, and brimming over with that love he'd never

dared hope to see again in the summer-blue of her eyes.
'All right, I'll marry you—on one condition...'

The giant stiffened, his golden frame leaning away
from her so he could look narrowly into her glinting
eyes, and Jessica held her face sober so he couldn't be
sure whether or not she was teasing him.

'OK,' he sighed after a moment. 'I'll fall for it—what's
the condition, Jess?'

'You carry me back to the yacht, since you had the
gall to throw me over! Well,' she taunted, wide-eyed and
innocent, when he looked completely taken aback, 'it's
you who claims god-like powers!' She began to giggle
nervously as he started to catch on. 'Colossus the First
would have carried me—no trouble!'

She was backing away, afraid even while she taunted
him, eyes twinkling with wicked mischief, the old Jessica
so thoroughly on view that Alec stood stock-still for a
moment, basking in the sight of her, clothes flattened
to her body and doing little to hide the beauty beneath,
hair like pale satin slicked to the perfect shape of her
head, cheeks glowing, mouth soft and full and red.

'A condition of marriage, Alec,' she thought fit to
remind him, wagging a finger at him in the same way
he had at her on the yacht earlier. 'It's you who claims
I want a god of my own to love, so...?'

His smile was rueful, all lopsided charm, and those
golden shoulders moved up and down in a submissive
shrug, then he began wading through the cool blue sea
towards her.

Jessica was just about to turn and begin swimming
when he caught her, and she squealed in terror as he
hoisted her easily up on to his shoulders, ignoring the
way she clutched at his hair, the way she shrieked to be
put down, begging him, eventually pleading with him

when the water reached his chest and her dangling feet. He took not the slightest bit of notice, continuing to walk slowly out into the bay until he was up to his chin in cool, clear water.

'Put me down now, Alec,' she pleaded with him. 'I take it back. I'll marry you, anyway—even if you aren't the god I thought you were,' she couldn't resist adding.

He had been about to let her go until she said that last bit, but his grip on her ankles tightened and on he went, walking himself right under the water, and in a fit of real panic Jessica struggled to get free, afraid of just how far he would go before conceding defeat, allowing herself to fall forwards into the water so he had to let her go.

Their heads bobbed up above the surface at the same time, both laughing, and Jessica went back into his arms as though she had never left them.

'I love you, Jess. I love——'

'No!' Her hand went up to cover his mouth, stopping the vow before it was firmly made. 'No need for words, darling,' she told him softly. 'Not any more. I don't need them, I only need you!'

Once upon a time, she had been content without hearing those special words, and she was again now. She had always known that Alec loved her. It had just taken him longer to accept it than she, that was all.

They swam back to the yacht together, Alec heaving himself out of the water first, then turning to help Jessica back on board.

'I have something to show you,' he told her as soon as her feet hit the wooden deck, and he took her hand, pulling her down the steps to the small cabin, letting go of her to duck down beneath the bench, coming up with a package in his hands.

He handed it solemnly to Jessica. 'Open it,' he urged. 'It's for you.'

Feeling breathless, Jessica fumbled with the paper wrappings, dragging them off the heavy package until she arrived at the box inside, then stopped, her fingers hovering over the infinitely familiar box. She glanced questioningly at Alec, but he just stood watching her gravely, giving nothing away, and she forced herself to look inside.

It was a bronze and gold-leafed statue of the Colossus. Jess held it tenderly in her hands, turning it this way and that, her heart full of emotion as she glanced back at Alec.

'The same one?' she enquired hoarsely.

Alec nodded. 'Christos Vangelis repaired him for me,' he told her gruffly. 'He did suggest that it might be better to buy a new one, but I wanted this one, damaged neck and all.' His voice had gone like gravel at the extent of his emotion. 'It's for you, Jess. I had him repaired to give back to you.'

Tears were clogging her throat, her hands trembling on the beautiful statue. 'No, Alec,' she choked. 'He's yours. I bought him for...'

'I have to earn him again,' Alec cut in flatly, pushing the statue back at Jessica when she tried passing it to him. 'I *want* to earn him honestly this time!'

'Then he belongs to neither of us,' she stated, gently sliding the statue back into its box. A strange smile crossed her face as she looked back up at Alec. 'Perhaps he never did. Perhaps I've been guilty of a terrible sin in expecting you to be something that you aren't, Alec... I'm sorry for that.'

Alec's body shook on an emotive sigh. 'We'll stand him in a place of honour in the apartment when we get home,' he decided. 'As a token of our love.'

'A lovely idea,' Jessica murmured, and went smoothly into his arms. After all, she thought privately, the Colossus belonged to the sun and the sky and the people of Rhodes. She had her own version here in her arms, and he was much more desirable than a mere graven image.

✦ Harlequin Romance ®

Coming Next Month

2995 SOME ENCHANTED EVENING Jenny Arden
Eve has to admit that Zack Thole is persistent, and wickedly
handsome, but she is almost committed to Greg and has no
intention of being carried away by moonlight and madness. Yet
Zack can be very persuasive....

2996 LORD OF THE LODGE Miriam MacGregor
Lana comes to New Zealand's Kapiti coast to find the father she's
never known, having discovered he works at the Leisure Lodge
guest house. Owner Brent Tremaine, however, completely
misinterprets her interest in his employee. Surely he can't
be jealous?

2997 SHADES OF YESTERDAY Leigh Michaels
Necessity forces Courtney to approach old Nate Winslow for help.
After all, Nate owes her something—her mother had said so—
though Courtney doesn't know what. So it annoys her that his son
Jeff regards her as an undesirable scrounger!

2998 LOVE ON A STRING Celia Scott
Bryony not only designs and makes kites, she loves flying them—
and Knucklerock Field is just the right spot. When Hunter Green
declares his intention to turn it into a helicopter base, it's like a
declaration of war between them!

2999 THE HUNGRY HEART Margaret Way
Liane has steered clear of Julian Wilde since their divorce. But when
Jonathon, her small stepson, needs her help, she just can't stay
away—even though it means facing Julian again. After all, it isn't as
if he still loved her.

3000   THE LOST MOON FLOWER
◯∾◯   Bethany Campbell   ◯∾◯

"Whitewater, I want you." These three desperate words not only
move lone hunter Aaron Whitewater to guide Josie through the
treacherous mountains of a tiny Hawaiian island to retrieve a
priceless stolen panda, they prove dangerously prophetic....

Available in August wherever paperback books are sold, or
through Harlequin Reader Service:

In the U.S.
901 Fuhrmann Blvd.
P.O. Box 1397
Buffalo, N.Y. 14240-1397

In Canada
P.O. Box 603
Fort Erie, Ontario
L2A 5X3

Harlequin Intrigue®

They went in through the terrace door. The house was dark, most of the servants were down at the circus, and only Nelbert's hired security guards were in sight. It was child's play for Blackheart to move past them, the work of two seconds to go through the solid lock on the terrace door. And then they were creeping through the darkened house, up the long curving stairs, Ferris fully as noiseless as the more experienced Blackheart.

They stopped on the second floor landing. "What if they have guns?" Ferris mouthed silently.

Blackheart shrugged. "Then duck."

"How reassuring," she responded. Footsteps directly above them signaled that the thieves were on the move, and so should they be.

For more romance, suspense and adventure, read Harlequin Intrigue. Two exciting titles each month, available wherever Harlequin Books are sold.